PRE

Withdrawing her ~~~~~~~~~~~~~~~~~~~~~~~
next to the bath, P~~~~ ~~~~ ~~~ second servant
that the jazz station he had just selected would
be more than adequate for her needs. When both
were gone, she locked the door, slid off her robe,
and removed the towel from her hair. She eased
herself into the bath, which felt heavenly, and
held her breath as she dunked herself, wetting
her hair.

Then she got out once more, put on her robe, and
orbed away in a shimmer of blue-white light.

She reappeared in her room in the Towers, a very
different kind of wardrobe laid out for her.
Phoebe and Piper had already changed, with
Chloe fussing about them, handling a few last-
minute details. The young woman didn't even
jump around an orb anymore, which was nice.
She had the makings of a truly terrific Wiccan.

"My alibi's in place," Paige said, tossing off her
robe and trying not to think about what she
might do if their imminent encounter did not go
as planned.

In moments she was dressing for war.

Charmed®

Published by Simon & Schuster

LUCK BE A LADY

An original novel by Scott Ciencin

Based on the hit TV series created by

Constance M. Burge

New York   London   Toronto   Sydney

To Denise, my eternal beloved
You cast a spell on me
Lucky that I am

SIMON SPOTLIGHT
An imprint of Simon & Schuster Children's Publishing Division
1230 Avenue of the Americas, New York, NY 10020
® & © 2004 Spelling Television Inc. All Rights Reserved.
All rights reserved, including the right of
reproduction in whole or in part in any form.
SIMON SPOTLIGHT is a registered trademark of Simon & Schuster.
The colophon is a trademark of Simon & Schuster.
Manufactured in the United States of America
First Edition 10 9 8 7 6 5 4 3 2 1
Library of Congress Control Number 2003108998
ISBN 0-689-85793-4

LUCK BE A LADY

Chapter

1

Phoebe leaned back in her nonergonomic desk chair and rubbed her tired eyes. She heard the purposeful tapping of keys from a workstation somewhere in the city room beyond her small office at the *Bay Mirror*, and felt a pang of guilt.

Well, it sounds like someone *at this newspaper is actually working*, she thought. *I just wish it was me.*

Lowering her hands, she allowed her stunning features to be bathed in the soft incandescence of the blank page displayed on her computer's flat-screen monitor.

That page was unforgiving. It was the enemy she had been wrestling with for hours. Lifting her wrist while suppressing a yawn, she checked her watch and saw that it was nearly eight o'clock at night. That meant she had been trying for the better part of five hours to get her advice column done, and it just wasn't happening.

In all fairness, it is *kind of hard to tell women what to do with their love lives when your own heart has been—forget broken—sliced and diced by the world's darkest and, okay, hottest demon.* She was anxious not only to console herself, but also to come up with a good reason for skipping out with her work undone.

She rummaged through the printouts of e-mailed letters addressed to "Ask Phoebe," squinting in her darkened office at the collection of complaints and wistful wishes from her readers, hoping to find just one that she could see her way clear to answering. They were all variations on the same theme.

Frowning, she read a few aloud. "How do I get him to notice me? How do I get him to love me? How do I get him to marry me?"

"Okay, Phoebe, *think,*" she whispered, setting her face in her hands.

Elise, her boss, had given her until high noon tomorrow to get her column in. Maybe if she waited until the morning, there would be some inspiration, something to jog her creative energy. Closing her eyes and attempting positive visualization, she tried to picture herself at 8 P.M. tomorrow with this week's column finally behind her.

I can't wait, she thought. Phoebe opened her eyes, shut down her computer, and grabbed her bag.

She didn't see the shadow crawling upon the

pebbled-glass window of her office door until it was too late. Hauling her door open, she thrust herself at the brightly lit city room beyond—

And nearly smashed into her ex-husband. A squeal of less-than-delighted surprise flying from her, Phoebe heard a sloshing and a fizzly hiss as something rocked from a cardboard container in his hands and threatened to spill. She looked down just in time to see two steaming Double-Mocha Surprises from the café downstairs tip forward, their lids sliding off, their dark, rich, and *really* hot contents leaping across the air in a wanton attempt to stain her brand-new silk blouse.

Cole drew in a breath—and the disaster in the making was suddenly *un*done. The splattering liquid drew itself back and *splooshed* right into the foam cups, which were leaning back into place, their lids sliding on and popping as they tightly sealed themselves shut.

Magic, Phoebe thought, recovering quickly. *Cole used his magic and he did it* here!

No one better have seen that!

From the newsroom, Phoebe heard someone deliver a surprised, "Gah!"

Swiveling to see beyond Cole's wide shoulders, Phoebe saw newsman George Phinnagee mopping up a "biggie" soda he had spilled on his desk, his computer, and himself as he chortled and snarled into his headset.

"No, no, I'm fine," he barked at someone on

the only lit phone line in the office. "A little accident, that's all. Just tell me the address. I'll remember it."

The middle-aged, balding reporter tossed the latest edition of the paper over the spill on the floor, and nodded several more times. "Right, good. Got it. Yeah, you bet I'll be there!"

Phoebe tore herself away. George was fine, and whatever was going on with him was none of her business. The rumpled, now soaking-wet reporter, in his ten-years-out-of-date tweed suit and matching hat, covered the crime beat, and he was the best there was at what he did.

"I guess everyone's got butterfingers around here," Cole said with a sly smile. "Lucky for us, I've got fast reflexes."

"Um-hmmm, lucky," Phoebe said disapprovingly. "I guess that's one word for it."

He hefted the drinks. "Got one for each of us. Your favorite, right?"

She nodded automatically.

Easing past her, he breezed into her office and set the drinks down on a table near her desk. Then he went back to the door, where she was moving aside, hoping he would just leave, and knowing things were never that easy with him.

"Well, you look"—he wanted to set the right tone—"well." He shrugged. "New blouse?"

"Yes, lucky it's still clean," Phoebe said pointedly. "Although I doubt luck had much to do with it."

Cole shot her a convincingly bemused look, then glanced back at George and his spilled soda, shifting his gaze to his own miraculously *not* spilled container, and back to Phoebe and her steely gaze. "Wait a minute. You think I . . ." He shook his head. "I didn't have anything to do with that. It was just coincidence."

"That's what you say. Maybe it's even what you believe. Who knows, it might even be the truth. But you need to face facts, Cole."

"And what facts might those be?" he asked in a soft, reassuring tone. It was his lawyerly voice, and it was one she had come to despise. He eased the door closed and shut it behind him, to keep George or anyone else who wandered by from hearing their conversation.

Phoebe threw up her hands in frustration. "You picked up so many powers in the demonic wasteland. That many powers were never meant to be all in the hands of just one person—if you are a person anymore. . . ."

"I am," Cole insisted. "Phoebe, I'm human. It's the human part of me that made it impossible for me to stay in that place, impossible to keep away from you. I—"

She raised a forefinger in warning. "Nah, uh-uh-uh! Don't you go starting with the 'L' word again, buster. I told you, it's over between us."

Cole shook his head. "Phoebe, it will *never* be over between us."

Phoebe drew a step back, vaguely threatened by Cole's insistence.

His shoulders slumped, undoing the sleek *GQ*-like lines of his dark gray, pinstriped designer suit. When they were together, her heart would flutter when he did that, because it made her picture him as a teenage boy standing at his prom date's front door, uncomfortable in his getup, unsure of what to do and say.

It made him seem *human*.

Cole sighed. "I'm just saying that feelings like the ones we have don't just go away. Not even when it would make things easier, or less painful, if they did."

"And I'm just saying that when it comes down to it, everything is cause and effect. You saved me some dry cleaning and a quick once over by Leo for minor coffee burns. Then, a second later, George nearly toasts his computer, and everything in the vicinity, with another spill. You prevent one problem over here, and cause another over there."

"Phoebe, my powers didn't do that."

"You don't know that for sure, do you?" she asked, delving deep. "You don't really have the first idea of what you're honestly capable of doing."

Now they were no longer just talking about magic.

"I'm getting really tired of asking this, but here goes," Phoebe said, steeling herself. "Cole, why are you here?"

He shrugged, but no longer looked youthful and disarmingly human. His expression was set. He was serious.

"All we need is *time*," Cole said urgently. "Time to give ourselves—no, us—another chance."

"It's not that easy and you know it."

"It's not easy at all," Cole said. "Loving someone never is."

Before Phoebe could say another word, Cole assumed his slightly wounded look—and teleported away, strange magical lines of power warping the space around him, then snapping out of existence too.

Phoebe turned, her gaze fixed on the presents Cole had brought. He was right, Double-Mocha Surprise was her favorite . . . or, it had been, until now.

Picking up the drinks as if they might bite her, Phoebe dumped them in the trash. Then she sat back down, booted up her computer, and typed away.

Dear Phoebe,

I once made a really big mistake. I fell for the wrong guy. I know, I know, you hear this all the time, but give me a chance to explain. This isn't your run-of-the-mill sob story.

See, the guy I fell in love with turned out to be a demon. Well, half demon. And he was working with evil forces out to destroy me and my two sisters.

Got your interest?

Good.

He was the love of my life. I gave up everything for him. My family, my friends . . . being a witch and one of the Charmed Ones . . .

I literally went to hell to become his bride.

Sure, eventually I came to my senses. Ever since then, I've done everything I can think to do to get rid of him. But nothing works.

I just want to say, "Hey, Cole, how can I miss you if you won't go away?"

No, wait, I have said that to him.

Like I said, nothing works. Nothing, but nothing. Nada. He just comes back, stronger and stronger, and he says he still loves me.

So what do I do? Is there even a little part of me that wants to give him another chance, despite everything he's done?

I don't think so. I want to say no.

The truth is.

The truth is . . .

"The truth is that I don't *know* what the truth is," Phoebe said, lifting her fingers from the keyboard and reaching over and turning off her computer without properly shutting it down.

She gathered her purse and the printouts of actual letters from readers needing help and swept out of her office, this time happy to note there were no surprises.

She worried for an instant that someone who

had seen Cole enter her office, yet never leave—at least not through the single door leading in and out—would wonder what was going on. But there was no one in the city room. No, that wasn't true. George was gone, but there were a couple of guys she didn't recognize at desks way in the back near the maintenance room, staring intently into computer screens. Interns, maybe. Junior researchers, possibly. They looked about college age, attractive, wearing leather jackets and jeans, and they were looking up stuff on the computer. It didn't appear that they had taken notice of Cole's mysterious exit.

Phoebe gasped as she felt her boot slide on something slick and wet!

She realized too late that she had walked onto the wet newspaper sopping up George's spilled drink. Her hand flew out and she managed to catch the edge of the reporter's desk just in time, narrowly avoiding a nasty fall on the slick floor. She leaned against the desk, cautiously let go of it, and felt her fingers absently grasp the headset George had been using.

A vortex opened in her mind.

Suddenly she was no longer in the city room. The vision that attacked her took Phoebe outside, to a small jetty overlooking the bay, somewhere down in the marina district. A collection of cloaked figures met upon a bizarre platform made of carved granite and marble stones that might have come from a cemetery. The platform itself was curved, with many tiers. Huge pieces of pipe jutted through the rock and transformed the sounds of the slow-moving water and generated a low, mournful kind of music.

Scanning the area, she spied Roman architecture: sturdy columns, ramparts, a dome . . .

Was she looking at something that had happened in the past?

A low horn sounded from a modern freighter cruising somewhere distant in the bay, its sound picked up and amplified by the "organ" that had been constructed nearby. No, she was looking at the here and now, or, more likely, the soon-to-be.

On the platform the cloaked figures, two dozen strong, threw back their hoods. Phoebe saw curved horns, scaly faces, diamond-sharp teeth, and glowing crimson eyes. Demons, all. Their mouths moved, but she could make out little of what they were saying. The names of certain crime-ridden districts in town drifted down to her, along with phrases in what sounded like arcane languages.

Then she sensed movement just off to her right. It was George, the crime reporter, bending low behind a rocky outcropping, a digital camera in his hands. He moved to position himself closer, to get a better shot, and rocks skittered and fell beneath his feet.

The demons turned, one spotting George. He opened his hand, and a spiral of flames leaped from his palm, engulfing the screaming reporter, who had no chance to run, no way to escape his terrible fate. . . .

Shuddering, Phoebe felt herself return to the comparatively mundane world of the newsroom. The two men she thought might be interns were on their feet, heading her way.

"I'm okay, I'm fine," Phoebe said, collecting herself and turning to face the new guys with a warm and confident smile that couldn't possibly have been more fake.

One of the guys was tall and lanky, with gray-blue eyes that reminded Phoebe of a cat. The other was shorter, his build fuller, like that of a bodybuilder, his hands small, but powerful looking.

"Are you sure you're okay?" the tall guy said as his companion scooped up a section of a recent paper from an adjacent desk and bent down to mop up more of the spilled soda.

"Sure, must be low blood sugar, long hours, you know how it is," Phoebe said jokingly. "No big deal."

"We could walk you to your car," said the shorter one, who had assigned himself to cleanup duty.

Phoebe smiled, this time calm and genuinely appreciative. The man kneeling before her also had gray-blue eyes. Could these two be brothers?

"I'll hit the candy machine on the way out," she said. "Half a chocolate bar and I'm good as new." It wasn't the first time Phoebe had to cover for her power to see visions of the future.

Stepping around the mess of soaked news-papers on the floor, Phoebe hurried away. She had to contact her sisters and warn them about what she had seen. There was an innocent to be saved and, from what little she had overheard of George's conversation with his informant earlier, very little time to spare!

Unknown to Phoebe, the two men from the newsroom watched her with icy gazes as she departed.

"Mr. Sigh," the tall one said softly.

The shorter man straightened up. "Mr. Tremble."

These were not their real names, of course. They were prevented from using their actual names due to a ruling by the Lords of the Outer Dark, whose dominion was absolute over all those in Sigh and Tremble's demonic clan.

Their family, once proud, once *rulers*, had been brought low. Now it was up to Sigh and Tremble to set things right.

"The reporter has no idea what he's walking into?" Mr. Tremble prompted.

"He does and he doesn't," Mr. Sigh replied. "The man I bribed to make the call gave him the time and location of a meeting between this city's *underworld* crime bosses. And that is the meeting he will attend. It was certainly a bit of good luck that the witch touched the phone as she did and received the premonition of danger."

"It would have been luckier for her if she had seen that we engineered this," Mr. Tremble observed.

"Lucky for us, she did not."

The tall man laughed. "We make our own luck."

"That we do."

Sigh and Tremble had great power over probabilities. Their demonic power allowed them to hand out or withdraw either good or bad luck, however they saw fit.

"What about the former Source?" Mr. Sigh asked. "He could be a problem for us. Even though he was vanquished by the Charmed Ones, he is back with even greater power."

"I agree; should he realize we are responsible for what is to happen tonight, there would be consequences. Yet we have been careful. The one we paid to make the phone call should be having a spot of bad luck any moment now, something involving an out-of-control bus, I believe. Have no worries, all is well."

"To vengeance," Mr. Sigh said, clasping his brother's arm.

Nodding triumphantly, Mr. Tremble returned the gesture and said, "To justice."

All was in readiness. Soon the Charmed Ones—and the demons who had brought Sigh and Tremble's clan low—would fall.

Chapter

2

Everything was quiet at P3, the nightclub Piper Halliwell owned and operated. And *that* was a problem. Club owners wanted crowds, excitement, and lots of noise. Those three things usually translated into an endless flow of cash emptying into their pockets.

Piper, a petite and elegant brunette, was smartly dressed in period-style 1940s clothing. She was, however—in her modest opinion—the picture of the twenty-first century club owner, confident and ready to strangle whoever had talked her into making tonight a theme night at the club when she could have booked some hot talent!

"I really think they're going to turn out for this," Leo said mildly, running his hand through his sandy hair sheepishly as he nodded toward the empty stage.

"Get that right from the Elders, didja?" Piper asked.

Leo, tall handsome dreamboat that he was— hard to believe he had actually died and been reborn as a Whitelighter, or guardian angel, over sixty years ago—looked genuinely perplexed. He straightened his knit turtleneck shirt, dragging it over his khaki pants.

The way Piper saw it, Leo was actually to blame for the debacle. A recent stop by their competitor, Destiny Lounge, had proven the other club's success with a sixties theme night. Leo suggested P3 try the same thing, using the forties instead, since it was where—or *when*—he'd spent his youth.

Except, Piper thought to herself, *what my dear husband didn't realize was that Destiny Lounge was hosting a reality show taping that night, which explains the crowd. And now P3 is empty, and I'm dressed like one of the Andrews Sisters!*

She stopped herself with a shudder.

I am a good witch, a good witch, a good witch, she chanted in her head. *I will not use my power to blow up my husband.*

Not unless he comes up with another bonehead idea like this one, she mentally amended.

Leo's brow furrowed at Piper's sarcastic tone. "Wait a minute, you can't blame me for this."

Piper's glare looked cold enough to freeze entire city blocks.

"Okay, obviously you *can* and you *do*," Leo said, "but that's not really fair, is it? Just because I had to orb into the Destiny Lounge across town, to help out a charge, and that place was, uh, *happening*, and I told you about it—"

Piper cut him off. "Never mind."

Leo looked deflated. "I'm sorry, Piper. I really thought if we recreated something like the old Hollywood Canteen it would be just like I remembered. Only I forgot that no one else would remember."

Piper knew another one of his war stories was on the way, and she really wasn't in the mood. They took place during World War II, in another era, another century from this one. And she hated to be reminded that he was technically dead. She was just thankful that he'd been given a second chance, and that it had been with her.

Leo tried to cheer them both up by swaying rhythmically to the song being played by the DJ. "'Boogie Woogie Bugle Boy,' one of the best ever written," he said. "It was nominated for an Academy Award in 1941. Bet you didn't know that."

"Thank you, Mr. Trivia."

"It wasn't trivia for me. That was only one year before . . ." He turned away.

One year before he lost his life in combat, Piper knew. "Okay, okay," she said, softening. "I didn't do enough to promote your idea. It was a self-fulfilling prophecy. I didn't think it would work, so I didn't put any effort into making it work. There, are you happy now?"

He looked back and delivered his most dazzling smile. "I'm always happy when we're together."

She melted.

She hated when he did that, made her melt. But she couldn't control her feelings for her husband. And she was learning that wasn't such a bad thing.

"It's not too late," Leo continued. "Like I said before, it could just be a case of everyone being too shy to be the first one on the dance floor. . . ."

Piper crossed her arms over her chest and shuddered. "No way, fella. You're not getting me up there."

"Oh, come on. Whatever happened to that old Coyote Piper spirit?"

"Spirit is just the word for it," Piper said quickly. "I wasn't even in my own body when that trampy ghost chick was bumping and grinding me up there."

"Yeah, but you looked *good*." He dragged out the last word, so that it sounded more like "gooooood."

"Aw, honey. That's sweet. Love you," she whispered.

"Me too."

"But I'm not doing it."

"It's a shame."

Before Leo could say anything else, a brunette blur bulleted down the stairs, stabbing her forefinger at various buttons on her cellular phone.

"I can't believe this," she hissed. "I *cannot* believe this."

"Saved by the Phoebe," Piper said, relieved.

Leo hummed a few bars of the DJ's latest selection, 'Sentimental Journey.' He did sound sweet, Piper had to admit. It was his favorite song of the era. Of course, there was that bit of Internet research she had done one time on the song, from which she learned that it actually hadn't been recorded until 1944, meaning Leo couldn't possibly have heard it before shipping out. Yet that was the way he remembered things, and it meant so much to him, she wasn't about to tease him about a failing memory over the song.

Phoebe swept over to them. "We've got a problem. I've been trying to call and give you guys the heads up about it the whole way here, but my cell phone keeps shorting out. I'm having the *worst* luck tonight!"

"Things haven't exactly been jumping around here," Piper complained, throwing Leo a look.

"So we have plenty of time to help an innocent," Leo said. "Should there be one or two, or . . ."

"Twelve," Piper interrupted.

Phoebe laid out the whole situation.

"The only problem is, I'm not exactly sure where we need to go," Phoebe said.

Leo laughed. "That's easy. The place you've

described has to be the Palace of Fine Arts, where they have the Exploratorium. That platform you saw was something called the 'Wave Organ.' I go there from time to time just to take in the sounds. You've got to be really still to appreciate them. It's a lot like . . ." He angled his head to the ceiling and made a couple of quick jerks.

"The place upstairs?" Phoebe asked.

"All the way upstairs," Leo answered patiently.

"Oh! Right. Wings and singing and soft mushy gooshy stuff," Phoebe said. "Not for me. I want the afterlife to be rockin'!"

"For you, I'm sure it will be," Leo said. He added quickly, "In a good way!"

"So where's Paige?" Phoebe asked. "From what I saw, this will probably need the Power of Three."

"She had that class tonight," Piper said.

"Well, let's go get her. I don't think we have any time to lose," Phoebe cautioned.

Piper nodded. For the first time tonight, she wished that she actually hadn't complained about things being a little quiet at the club.

Pretty soon now she was going to have all the action she could handle.

Paige Matthews, half sister to Piper and Phoebe, and half Whitelighter to boot, sat in a tiny desk chair at the local community collége, taking a night course in genealogy.

Ugh! Who thought there'd be so much work involved?

The stunning redhead sat staring down at the crazy quilt of notes she'd scrawled all over the handouts her teacher had given at the beginning of class. The notes went up one side of a page, down another, and sometimes formed concentric rings that spiraled into the tiniest print she could manage.

It wasn't that Paige had anything against study and hard work. Until a few months ago, she'd been employed as a social worker.

Since then she had devoted herself almost entirely to the complex study of the magical arts, and she had loved every minute. She had signed up for this course, on the other hand, for fun.

Or . . . she might have had another reason or two.

The small classroom was half empty, and Paige wondered if her instructor, a tall, sour-faced man who wore honest-to-goodness tweed, had been taking out his frustration over the poor enrollment on the students who'd made the mistake of actually coming here tonight. Her teacher, the aptly named Louis Lasher, was busy making a complicated chart on the blackboard. Paige knew she should have been trying to get the drop on the man and copy down every name and mark that he was making even as he made it, and, in that way, been ready once he started talking a mile a minute.

But if she did that, she wouldn't be able to steal as many glances at the gorgeous Asian-American guy seated next to her. He was young, athletic, and blessed with male-model features.

"Ben Kwatsai," he said, without looking her way.

Paige recoiled, one eyebrow raised. She stared openly now, and saw that he was smiling.

"I'm a phys ed instructor," he said softly. "It pays, in my line of work, to develop excellent peripheral vision."

"Oh," Paige said. "You caught me peeking."

"I did, yes."

"And you're okay with that?"

"Yes."

Paige was already feeling better about this class. "I'm looking to find out more about my family."

"Me too. I only recently found out I was adopted and—"

Their teacher spun on them with a bright red face and crimson ears. "If the two of you aren't here to learn, I suggest you carry on your flirtations elsewhere."

Ben nodded, considering that. Partially covering his mouth, he said to Paige, "I've already picked up everything he's outlining on the Internet and I could teach it to you faster. Care to come to the student library with me?"

"Delighted."

Ben packed up his things, Paige following suit. Within minutes they were walking across campus, still laughing about the tirade Mr. Lasher went on when they announced they actually *were* leaving. If they listened very, very hard, they could still hear him in the distance.

The library was spacious, yet also sparsely populated. Ben and Paige sat at a long table upon which a dozen computer terminals had been set. The crimson-haired witch was impressed as she watched Ben's long, lithe fingers breeze across the keyboard, displaying a grace she wouldn't have expected, considering his stated profession. His confidence was compelling. She saw several other young women looking at him.

Shoo! Scat! she thought, wishing them away. *He's mine.*

"I know what it's like to have two families," Paige said, feeling completely comfortable with this man, as if they were not strangers at all. "When I was growing up, I always used to tune out whenever people started talking about aunt-this-person or granddad-that-person, and now—"

"Now you want to know, but there's really no one to ask."

She nodded, and soon found herself answering a handful of questions about her past. Ben had logged on to several sites to which he'd had to give password identification, and he explained that he had paid fees to each site for records access.

"It's all perfectly legal," Ben said. "This is just a matter of taking advantage of the shortcuts people out there can provide."

"Great," she said brightly, unsure of what else she could say. Her instincts told her that in every conceivable way, this guy was perfect for her . . . which was crazy, of course. She'd only just met him!

"Let me work on this for another second or two," Ben said, his fingers tapping away. "I think we might just get lucky."

"I think I already have," she whispered, fighting the impulse to rest her face on his impressively muscled shoulder.

He smiled, acknowledging her statement without calling any more attention to it than that, and sat back. "Here."

Paige tore her gaze away from Ben and focused on the screen. He had pulled up a clipping from an old Los Angeles newspaper. Her mouth opening silently, Paige allowed her hand to close over his forearm. She felt a need to anchor herself as she took in the image staring back at her from the screen.

It was her!

Or rather, the woman in the photo from the World War II-era story looked just like her, only with a different do and clothes that must have been the cat's meow back in their day.

"She looks like a movie star," Paige said, awed.

"She was, according to this."

"Really?"

"'Penny Day Matthews,'" Ben read from the article, "'signed today with Osiris Studios to star in their feature *Star-Spangled Nights*, a romantic extravaganza celebrating our boys at war and the women who love them.'"

"So she was my . . . what?" Paige asked, curious about her connection to this glamorous dame!

"From what I saw before I got to this screen, she was your great-aunt on your adoptive father's side."

Paige sat back in confusion. "But that doesn't make any sense. She looks just like me. How could that be, when I was adopted into the family?"

"The past is a mystery," Ben said quietly. "Mine certainly is. I'm trying to find out everything I can about my birth parents before I decide if I want to go see them or not. I think my grandparents were in an internment camp during the war. What effect that had on my birth parents, if it contributed to them giving me up . . . I just don't know. But I want to find out. I've always found it's best to know everything you can about a person before you let them fully into your life."

"Come on," Paige said, knocking his powerful arm with hers. She felt him slipping away, their personal connection threatening to fade as he apparently reminded himself of the importance of the idea he had just voiced. "You don't believe in chance? Or that some things were meant to be?"

"I'm not sure."

"What about luck? You mentioned luck before?"

He smiled, and unexpectedly took her hand and kissed it, like a knight from a King Arthur flick. "Luck be a lady, they say."

Feeling her heart threatening to thunder right out of her chest, Paige was trying to come up with some reasonable rejoinder when she spotted her sisters and Leo hurrying her way. Phoebe was shooting daggers into her cellular phone with her eyes, while Piper was rolling hers.

"Paige, hi," Leo said, taking the initiative. "Could we see you for a minute?"

Studying the Whitelighter's patent "There's trouble, we need you" look, Paige sighed inwardly.

Reaching over, she pulled up a notepad program on the computer and typed in her phone number.

"Call me?" she asked Ben.

"I'd be a fool if I didn't," he assured her. "And I'm no fool."

A minute later they were outside. "You weren't in class," Piper said. "Good thing Leo can sense you!"

"Well, I'm here now. What's up?" Paige asked.

Leo and the other Charmed Ones quickly brought her up to speed.

"The place will be closing soon," Leo said. "I figure the demons either bribed or knocked out the security guards on duty. That would explain why they were able to gather at the spot Phoebe saw in her vision."

"I thought they liked parking garages and dark alleys or deserted warehouses," Paige said, still not altogether thrilled to have her evening with Ben cut short, though she knew her responsibilities as a Charmed One would always come first.

"There's a possibility of mystical confluence

on that spot," Leo said. "It may be why the music there is so beautiful, and so soothing to the soul—"

"Soothing and beautiful, right," Piper cut in. "Bottom line: demons, bad; demons gathering in a place of power, even worse; and an innocent needing to be saved from a whole gaggle of demons who really won't be glad to see us, about as bad as things can get."

"What do we know about these guys?" Paige asked, looking around to ensure that the darkened spot near the hedges around the back of the administrative building was indeed deserted and far enough from prying eyes for what they needed to do. "The demons, I mean."

Leo filled her in, while Phoebe finally abandoned her apparently cursed cellular phone and dumped it into her oversized purse. She fished out a couple of potions and spells she had hastily prepared, since she was sure there was a demon behind ths somehow.

"We tried calling you. None of our cell phones work," Phoebe said. "I'm thinking there may be a curse."

Piper shrugged. "Or we've all been so busy we've been forgetting to recharge the batteries."

Paige reached out for her sisters' hands. "Well, I'm feeling pretty charged up. Let's do this!"

Leo nodded, and with that, all four figures were engulfed in a radiant shimmer of blue-white light . . . and were gone.

Chapter

3

Leo stood alone in the darkness near the water, waiting for reporter George Phinnagee to arrive at the spot Phoebe had foreseen in her vision. He ached to be at his wife's side. Piper, Phoebe, and Paige had taken up positions flanking the still-gathering lot of robed demons on the curving oblong stone shelves that made up the greatest part of the unique wave organ. His fondest desire was to protect the woman he loved, but he knew, as he had always known, that he would do more harm than good to the natural order of things if he yet again attempted to circumvent the will of the Elders—and that of fate itself—by attempting to put himself between Piper and harm's way.

Though he had died more than sixty years ago, having to make this choice each time, to stand back and guide, to support, to remain levelheaded when tempers flared or passions rose, often felt like dying all over again.

Not to say that Piper was anything close to helpless. She was one of the three most powerful witches in existence, and her power, and the bond they shared, had saved *him* just as often as his level execution of his duties had saved her.

Yet . . .

When he had been a medic, a healer, during the Big One, the Second World War, the enemy he had battled was injury, disease, and death. Since his own time, he had been reborn as a Whitelighter, a guardian angel for witches, other potential Whitelighters, and people whom the demon world had targeted because of the good they had done, or might yet do, in their current lives.

In his second life he had battled darkness and evil in every conceivable form long before he had been given the Charmed Ones as his charges. He had saved so many lives, not only by gently guiding those he cared for away from evil and its endless temptations, but also by kicking demon butt when necessary.

Tonight he could *feel* the powerful forces radiating from the bodies of the cloaked figures. These were mid- and upper-level demons, creatures with the power to draw strength and mystical energies from the living, the dead, and the Earth itself. It was no wonder that they had chosen this spot for their meeting. This structure served as a focus, or amplifier, of more than just nature's soothing sounds from the water; it also increased the magical potentiality of any who stood in its apex . . . and the forces they might unleash.

Put simply, it was dangerous as all hell.

A rustling came, and Leo looked over from the dark, damp arroyo he had chosen as his place of concealment. The man in the tweed suit was unusually agile and stealthy, though his clothing did make him stand out.

The reporter had arrived.

Inwardly hoping Piper and the others were ready, Leo surged ahead, grabbing the reporter from behind, one hand encircling his chest and pinning in place the arm that was reaching for his camera, the other closing over the man's mouth to prevent him from crying out and drawing the attention of the gathered demons.

"Trust me, if you knew what was really going on, you'd thank me," Leo said.

With those words he orbed out with the reporter, the chiming sound that accompanied the act of teleportation sounding, for some reason, higher, shriller, less like chimes than screams.

Phoebe drew a sharp breath as the demons turned in the direction of the shimmering orb streaks left behind by Leo's quick rescue and disappearing act. She and her sisters were on the other side of the platform, crouching in something wet and squishy that wasn't being merciful on any of their outfits or shoes. Such was the life of fighting evil.

True, they could have just spirited off the innocent and left these demons to whatever business they had planned, but something big and bad was going down here. This many demons didn't get together for any other reason.

One strange thing, though. This time Phoebe had been able to make out more than just snippets of what the demons had been talking about. Yes, they were mentioning crime-ridden territories throughout San Francisco, and it appeared each of them ruled a supernatural crime syndicate in those territories. But they had been arguing over who had called this meeting and why, not one stepping forward to take the credit or the blame. Had this get-together been arranged by someone else?

If so, why?

"Time for action," Piper whispered. "Remember what Leo said, any magic that we do here will be increased ten times at least. That could be why they're meeting here, because any attacks on one another might mean blowing themselves up. So pick your targets carefully and be prepared for the results."

"Aye, aye, Sergeant Piper," Paige said with a toss of her red hair and a mock salute. "Sheesh!"

The three sisters broke from cover, Phoebe leaping and levitating onto the platform just as the hooded demons turned to face her. She threw down an all-purpose demon vanquishing potion, then back-flipped in midair, narrowly avoiding a sweeping sword that had been produced from beneath the closest demon's robes. She landed back where she had started, her sisters chanting a spell of protection as the small glass vial containing the potion shattered at the epicenter of the demon gathering. The potion ignited and a violet shield rippled into existence between the sisters and the mayhem that was about to erupt. There was a thunderclap accompanied by a blinding burst of reddish amber and pure white energies. Two demons were engulfed and incinerated while others were lifted into the air and the rest were scattered by the blast's force. The shield protecting the sisters buckled, the force of the magical destruction the Charmed Ones had unleashed proving even greater than any of them had expected, but it held.

The worst of the first-wave attack behind them, Piper and Paige collapsed the shield and leaped into the fight, Phoebe right behind them.

"Hey, tall, dark, and horny!" Phoebe hollered at a dazed demon as he turned his ugly, scaly face in her direction, his curling horns glinting in the moonlight. *Heh. Always wanted to say that,* she thought. "Try some of this on for size!"

Phoebe delivered a sweeping roundhouse kick that caught the demon under its smelly snout with a resounding *crack*. Its head whipped backward and it stumbled toward another of its kind just as Piper moved forward and raised both hands.

"Fire in the hole, people!" Piper yelled.

Phoebe and Paige dove for cover as Piper gestured, flicking her wrists, and the two demons who had stumbled into each other exploded with enough force to rock the entire platform!

Phoebe spun as she saw a wave of demon debris scatter, including razor-sharp teeth and jutting shards of bone, flying out at dizzying speed.

"And freeze," Piper said, gesturing again. This time, every demon on the platform—and the frightening wave of what was left of the demons Piper had vanquished—froze as if someone had hit the pause button on a VCR's remote control. Piper was unaffected, ditto with her sisters.

The petite brunette joined Phoebe and Paige, and all three slipped behind a rock. Piper was about to gesture again to unfreeze the demons when Paige stopped her.

"Wait up," Paige said, one hand on Piper's wrist.

"I've ruined a perfectly good pair of shoes over this, I'm not good with waiting," Piper said briskly. She moved to unfreeze the tableau again and Paige bounced excitedly as she knelt next to her.

"Hold up!" Paige pleaded. "Listen, your powers don't usually work like that. A vanquish is a vanquish, right? Maybe a little demon dust to clean up, not a big rocketing mass of *ewww*, right?"

"Who knows?" Piper answered. "Must have to do with the amplification factor. As long as they're dead and it's not in my living room, I don't care."

Phoebe assessed the current situation. "Maybe we could just take them out while they're still frozen there. It's easier when they don't fight back."

"Maybe," Piper said. "But where's the fun in that?"

Piper flicked her wrists and they heard screams and more demons falling as the debris whipped through several of the cloaked figures who were still standing.

Paige jumped out from cover. "Fine, I want to see what I can do, then." Holding out one open palm, she commanded, "Sword!"

Shimmering, one of the demon's swords dematerialized out of its hand and rematerialized in Paige's hand so fast she almost didn't have time to wrap her fingers around its hilt. Fortunately her reflexes also felt heightened in this place, and she grabbed the sword just in time, angling it down and before her.

"And back atcha!"

The sword shimmered, vanished, and reappeared in the chest of the demon she had snatched it from. With a roar of pain, he fell back, smacking to the platform's surface.

Phoebe joined in the fight, punching and kicking with greater force than she had ever known. Still, something felt not quite right here. Somehow this was just too easy.

She shrugged, using a far less powerful potion to vanquish another demon.

It was possible that the mystical confluence in this spot had a vested interest in the side of good, and that's why this was going so well.

Or maybe, finally, their luck was changing.

"This isn't where I meant to go," Leo said, confused by the sight of the black shale cave and the flickering golden torches set in braziers on the wall. The reporter shrugged off his grip and turned to face Leo. Slipping off the tweed hat, the man Leo had orbed to this strange place looked at him with piercing gray-blue eyes.

"Bad luck, I suppose," the man said, shucking off the jacket, too. Leo could now see that it had been ill-fitting. The man smiled. "Don't worry about it. Everyone gets a run of bad luck eventually."

This man was younger than Phoebe had described, and with a full head of straw-colored hair. He also looked very fit, his white shirt almost bursting against the thick slabs of muscle that made up his chest and arms.

"Wait a minute," Leo said warily, realizing he had grabbed the wrong man. "Who are you? I don't understand. . . ."

The man with the gray-blue eyes smiled. "Anyone can change the future, not just you and the Charmed Ones."

"You're not him. You're not George, the reporter." Leo took a step back, looking around for anything he could use as a weapon.

"You're not wrong," the man said. "You can call me Sigh. Mr. Sigh. Though, by the time this night is done, I'll be able to give my true name once more. I'm magically forbidden, you see. My tongue would turn to acid if I tried to say my actual name."

With that, the man gestured, and his wardrobe changed. Suddenly he was dressed in tight black slacks and boots, sporting a tight black long-sleeved turtleneck and a golden necklace with a shining amulet in the shape of a pentagram.

He was a demon.

"There was so much evil in that place," Leo said, putting some pieces of the puzzle together. "That's why I couldn't single you out."

"That was the idea, yes."

Leo tried to orb out, but the shimmering light that rose about him faltered and faded away three times. He didn't understand. . . . He'd been able to orb into this place easily enough. Why couldn't he orb out?

Leo quickly surveyed the rocky chamber. It looked as though there had been tunnels leading out of here, but a recent rockfall had blocked them all. He had no way out.

He was trapped.

Flexing his short, but powerful-looking hands, the demon circled Leo. "My brother and I knew you wouldn't be able to resist the bait we had laid out for you and the lovely ladies. An innocent to save? Demons to vanquish? A perfect trap for the Charmed Ones and their Whitelighter."

"Why did you do all this? What happened to the reporter?"

"Oh, he's fine. He had three flats on the way over here. What luck, huh?"

"What's going to happen to Piper?"

"You have more important things to worry about," Mr. Sigh whispered, flicking his wrists and laughing as a pair of shining silver bolts shot out from apparatus strapped to his forearms beneath his long-sleeved shirt. "I took these bolts from the crossbows of Darklighters who encountered a series of unfortunate events that led to their very messy demises. Again, bad luck, you might say. For them."

Leo shook his head. There was nothing more important to him than protecting his beloved wife and his other charges, not even safeguarding his own existence. As the demon came running at him in the confined space, the deadly tips of the bolts shining in the torch-lit chamber that showed no possible exits, he shouted, "Piper! Paige!"

He was reaching out with his power, hoping to get a message through along the same channel that allowed him to hear his charges when they called him. He thought Paige, at the very least, might hear him, considering she was part White-lighter.

"Anyone?" Leo demanded.

Then the demon was on him.

Hidden by a cloak of shadows, Mr. Tremble watched the battle upon the strange platform. The Charmed Ones fought with abandon, actually enjoying the conflict, testing the new levels of their might with great relish. What they hadn't yet noticed was that for every demon they vanquished, another was suddenly just *there* to take his place. That, of course, was because of the nature of the demons they fought, and of the very thing that was increasing everyone's powers during this fracas: the location itself. The Lords of the Outer Dark were drawing on the power of this place to increase their own parasitic abilities.

In other words, the more sheer power the Charmed Ones unleashed, the more power the demons were draining from the witches and using that power to reconstitute themselves and grow stronger after each vanquishing. It was a fight the Charmed Ones could not win, simple as that. On the other hand, the witches possessed more power than the greedy Lords of the Outer Dark could handle. And so, very soon, the Charmed Ones would be drained and destroyed, and the Lord of the Outer Dark would be over-loaded and destroyed.

The main worry that Mr. Tremble had enter-tained was the possibility that their Whitelighter would see the true danger and orb them away in time. Thus Mr. Sigh had taken Leo out of play. Of course, that left the half-Whitelighter, Paige, who could also orb once one of them understood what was happening.

Drawing an ancient, silver pistol from beneath his coat, Mr. Tremble raised it and took aim at Paige. Gathering his power, he drew in a breath and fired, an arcane word leaving his lips as the bullet left his gun.

Paige groaned, her head flung back, as the bullet grazed her temple and sent her uncon-scious form to the ground. Both remaining sis-ters gasped as they saw Paige fall, and while they clearly wished to race to their sister's side, the demons they were facing weren't about to let that happen. Taking advantage of Phoebe and Piper's distraction, the demons landed punish-ing physical and mystical blows on the young women, forcing them to face the demon horde without knowing if their half sister was alive or dead. That made Phoebe and Piper fight more fiercely *and* more recklessly, and thus, this mat-ter would quickly come to a head. Mr. Tremble would make sure that Paige would revive just in time for one last incantation of the Power of Three. And then they would all be consumed.

Excellent. That would be exactly the outcome the tall Mr. Tremble had engineered.

"Lucky shot," said a husky voice behind him.

Mr. Tremble spun and was surprised to see Cole Turner, the former demon Belthazor, once the Source of All Evil, standing before him in a designer suit.

"You weren't supposed to be here," the lanky demon said as he took Cole's measure.

"Well, I am," Cole said, ready for a fight.

"Probabilities are a complex business. Rogue elements are never welcome."

"You and my ex-wife," Cole groused, "*always* telling me where I'm not wanted!"

Cole materialized a fireball in his hand, yanked it back, and hurled the roaring mass of magical energy at Mr. Tremble!

Whooosh!

Except . . . Cole's foot had slipped on a rock at the last second, his aim had been thrown off just a touch, and the fireball had sailed to one side and gone far beyond Mr. Tremble, catching one of the demons fighting the Charmed Ones and destroying him instantly.

A backlash was instantly felt as a shockwave of mystical fires reached out like a crackling orange-and-crimson scythe. Piper and Phoebe both slipped and fell at exactly the right moment so that the scythe whipped out and over their heads, narrowly avoiding them—what luck—as it ripped through *all* the demons upon the platform.

Mr. Tremble faded into the shadows, smiling as he recalculated the possibilities and probabilities. Taking it all into consideration, he knew full well that even with this intrusion, he had won; his work here was done. He saw Cole begin to turn, looking to engage him in combat, certainly, and he quickly dematerialized, unable to restrain his laughter.

Piper rushed to Paige, who was already stirring. "She's all right," Piper announced. "She's going to be fine. Leo? Leo!"

Seconds passed, and Leo did not materialize. "That's strange," Piper said warily.

"Yeah, and it's not the only thing," Phoebe commented as she turned her attention to her former husband. "Cole! What are you doing here?"

Straightening his tie, Cole leaped onto the platform. "Making myself useful. What does it look like?"

"Were you *following* me?"

"Right now, does it really matter?"

"Yes! I want to know."

Cole grimaced. "Fine. I *felt* that you were in trouble. Don't ask me how. And I just knew where to find you."

For an instant Phoebe thought this was a manifestation of another of Cole's otherworldly powers, possibly even some offshoot of so many strange abilities that were never meant to coincide, all working together to make Cole into something more than demon or human.

Piper clearly had another idea. Her face went pale as she said, "*Leo*. It must have been Leo somehow!"

"But why wouldn't he come himself?" Phoebe asked.

Cole nodded upward. "Maybe he got a call from the Elders. Dunno."

Laying on her back, Paige gestured weakly toward the area behind her sisters. "Company," Paige whispered.

Phoebe spun and saw that the demons who had been vanquished were all reforming and coming *back* to life.

"Okay, this isn't good," Piper said worriedly. "Leo, get your butt over here *now*!"

Phoebe and Cole helped lift Paige to her feet, and within moments all four faced a horde of cloaked demons who encircled them.

"Paige, orb us out . . . now!" Piper demanded.

Her head lolling, Paige said, "Can't . . . can't concentrate, can't do it yet. . . ."

"All right, then let me," Cole said. He lifted one hand, as if to perform a mystical gesture, but Phoebe stopped him, her hand clamping down on his arm.

"No, thanks," Phoebe said firmly. "No demonic magic."

Cole's eyes widened in frustration. "Phoebe, I keep telling you, I'm not evil anymore!"

"Even if you're not, your powers are," Piper chimed in. "Phoebe's right. We took these guys down once, we can do it again."

"Fine," Cole said, calling up another fireball. "If that's the way you want it, let's vanquish these guys so they stay vanquished!"

Leo fought for his life against the muscular demon. So far he'd been lucky, managing to dodge and dart at just the right times to avoid the shining silver bolts stripped from a Darklighter's crossbow, but he had the feeling that was exactly how the demon wanted things. His enemy was toying with him, taking his time and enjoying that he had an emissary of good on the ropes.

"We've been planning this for a very long time, Whitelighter," Mr. Sigh said as his deadly bolts swept close enough to slice into Leo's shirt, but not graze his flesh. "Those demons your precious Charmed Ones are fighting are all that stand between my clan and the power that should rightfully be ours—instead of the shame and exile that's been forced on us."

"Exile and shame, huh?" Leo said, leaping back, again looking for *anything* he could use as a weapon. "That's got to suck. These guys have a name?"

Mr. Sigh grinned broadly. "Your optimism amuses me. You honestly think there's a chance you'll get out of here alive and be able to help your charges. It will never happen."

"So humor me. You seem to be all chatty anyway."

The demon drove one of the bolts into a section of rock right next to Leo's head. Only a last-second feint had saved the Whitelighter. Grabbing the demon's other arm, Leo twisted it back, heard a satisfying *snap*, and stomped down on his opponent's instep. Mr. Sigh screamed and Leo darted off as the demon freed his right hand from the rock wall and brought that bolt across at Leo's face in a wide sweep of the weapon.

But Leo was quick, easily evading the angry arc of the weapon. The demon shook his broken arm, and the crackling that resulted echoed in the chamber. He brought his arm up, showing that it was no longer injured.

"Nice trick," Leo said, dancing back several yards, safe from harm. For now. "So, come on. Tell me about these guys who've been running roughshod over your clan."

"They're the Lords of the Outer Dark," Mr. Sigh said, his expression no longer so ebullient as he stalked toward his prey. "And only warriors with the power of the Charmed Ones could hope to destroy them. Of course, in the battlefield we selected, the release of mystical forces is bound to be so great that none stand any chance of surviving."

"And you're keeping me here so I can't orb them out of danger at the last second," Leo said, circling to avoid his attacker.

"Precisely. And the half-Whitelighter, Paige, has also been dealt with."

Dealt with. Leo didn't like the sound of that one bit. He had to figure out a way to beat this guy. In a fair fight Leo could have taken the lanky demon easily. But with his weapons and his reach, the demon had the advantage here.

One thing still didn't make sense. He had been able to orb into this chamber easily enough. Why couldn't he just orb out again? Admittedly he had been in similar situations before, yet there was usually some reason for him to become trapped.

He gasped as enlightenment struck him. He suddenly had a hunch about what to do, and right now he had so little time, playing that hunch felt like his only option.

"Well, okay," Leo said, raising his hands in surrender. "I guess you've got me."

"I know you don't believe that," the demon said, surging forward. "I know you have something planned. It doesn't matter. I will—"

Leo leaped at the demon, grabbing both of his wrists and forcing them away from him to either side as he delivered a crushing forehead smash that stunned his opponent, and a hard knee to the center of his chest that folded him over and made the demon collapse against him.

"We were touching when we orbed here the first time," Leo said.

This time he tried orbing again—and the

blue-white streaking lights took him away, their chimes sounding heaven-sent . . . as well they *should*.

"What do they feed you guys?" Phoebe asked as she delivered a knife-edged thrust with her open hand, fingers pressed together, to the throat of yet another demon. It gurgled and stumbled back.

"Us, I think," Cole said, having exchanged fireballs for lightning strikes, and coiling streams of pure darkness that crushed the life out of a victim. The power flowed through him, the demons fell . . . but it wasn't enough. They just kept coming back. "They're feeding on *us*!"

"Phoebe . . . ," Paige whispered, still weak, but holding her own as she repeated her earlier trick of orbing demonic weapons from the hands of attackers then right back into their chests. "Let Cole take us out of here. He's right. I can feel it too."

Piper was sweating, her legs about to buckle beneath her as she exploded one demon after another, the creatures reforming practically on the spot. "My vote's for Cole, though I can't believe I'm saying it."

"We haven't tried a Power of Three spell," Phoebe insisted.

"It's dangerous," Cole said, taking down another demon. "There's something about this place that can make anything happen. I haven't felt a presence like this for a long time."

"Power of Three," Phoebe said. "And if that doesn't work, Cole can take us away."

"All right," Piper hissed.

"Ready," Paige added uneasily.

"I'll keep them back," Cole said, raising a sparkling crimson-and-amber shield around them that he knew the demons would be able to shatter in less than a minute. No problem.

That was all the time they needed . . . and more.

Phoebe unfolded a small piece of paper and held it before her as Piper took her hand, then Paige's.

"Demons in darkness cloaked—by the Power of Three, we'll see you croaked!" they hollered, Phoebe inwardly wincing at her bad poetry. It was all she could come up with in that tiny bit of time she had to prepare!

Anyway, it seemed to be doing the trick. The witches chanted the incantation twice, thrice, and Cole allowed the shield to fall as a buildup of mystical energies flashed from the sisters, lighting them as if from the inside with blinding bursts of fiery light.

"That's not supposed to happen," Cole said.

"No, it's not," called a familiar voice from the darkness beyond the platform. Leo was back, shrugging off a semiconscious luck demon who looked a little like the one Cole had faced just before the demons had regenerated. "Piper, stop the spell!"

It was too late. The eyes of the three witches were now completely enveloped by mystical energies. They were in a trance, creating a mystical flame that was spiraling outward, threatening to engulf everyone and everything in sight.

"Cole, get them out of there!" Leo called. "I can't orb them in this state. We don't know what would happen."

"How do I make them stop?"

Leo shook his head. "I don't know!" he hollered over the roaring wind that was rising with the magical maelstrom. "Try to redirect the energies. Do whatever you have to! Just take them somewhere safe!"

Cole nodded, walking into the midst of the chanting witches, ignoring the hooded demons who burst apart, reconstituted, shattered, exploded, imploded, and kept coming back to life.

The destruction never touched him, which, in itself, could be taken as proof of his incredible power.

Calling upon one of the abilities he had ripped from a vanquished demon on the other side, Cole opened a swirling vortex of energy large enough to consume the three Charmed Ones and spun it high over their heads, willing it with all his strength to absorb the power they were releasing. He hoped it would take them someplace safe.

Just as he had earlier, he *felt* Leo's distant presence touching his consciousness.

Safe, safe, somewhere safe, keep them safe, Leo's voice chanted.

No argument from me, Cole thought, desperate to ensure Phoebe made it out of this alive. Saving her sisters would be icing on the cake, but they took a backseat to protecting her.

As if he sensed Cole's intent, Leo's voice grew more insistent, and flickers of memory from the Whitelighter reached into Cole's mind, and from there, into the vortex as it came crashing down upon the Charmed Ones, its form buckling, unable to contain their power. Cole came closer, entering the vortex and adding all the power that was at his command to saving the witches as he touched Phoebe's face, the power flying from her so strong it might have burned him to a cinder if he had been human. Or demon, for that matter.

The cloaked demons on the platform grew as they took in all the power they could, then blew apart in a final conflagration of mystical energies, the Lords of the Outer Dark unable to contain the power they had taken from the witches and this place.

On the sand just two dozen feet away from the stony rise, Leo watched as the vortex Cole had called into existence shimmered in the midst of the explosion loosed by the dying demon horde.

Then, just as suddenly as the battle had begun, it was over, all traces of the demons, Cole, or the Charmed Ones gone.

Leo turned to grab at the luck demon who had been a part of setting all this up, but the demon was gone. He reached out with his power and attempted to feel where Piper had wound up and fear closed on him like the fist of a giant, ancient god. He *couldn't* sense her. She wasn't anywhere on Earth, nor anywhere in the realms above or below that he could sense.

"Piper!" he screamed, a flood of images of him living his life without his beloved hitting him hard. *"Piper!"*

It did him no good.

Piper and her sisters were gone.

Chapter 4

Gunfire erupted all around the three witches and their companion as they tumbled from the already disappearing vortex to a sandy shore on a windswept, overcast day. Great dunes of gusting white sand surrounded them, rough waves roaring and biting at a nearby beach.

"Where are we?" Phoebe whispered. "And what time is it?" Just then the labored grunts of frantic, determined men drifted their way, along with the hiss of sand shifting beneath heavy boots.

Soldiers who looked confused but very dangerous appeared, then halted on either side of the foursome.

On one side stood a whole bunch of guys in *Saving Private Ryan* wear: dark green helmets, brown and green fatigues, and heavy dark boots, with M1 carbines and M1903 rifles cradled in their arms. Americans. The group of enemy soldiers they were up against wore gray and black and were also armed with rifles.

Nazis.

"Leo!" Piper yelled. "Leo, get us out of here. Now!"

Their guardian angel did not materialize.

"Where'd tha dames come from?" a Nazi asked, his accent suspiciously tinged with Brooklynese.

An Ally leveled his weapon and called, "What do we do?"

"Whoa, whoa, whoa, whoa—whoa!" Piper stammered. "Don't do anything! Don't shoot!"

She was about to freeze them all when someone yelled, "Cut!"

The soldiers on both sides disassembled as a clomping came from the other side of a dune. A man appeared atop the rise, megaphone in hand. He wore thick round black glasses, a white shirt with wide sleeves rolled up to his forearms, a flapping tie, and thick suspenders leading down to his tan flared breeches and black riding boots.

"Who are you ladies and why are you ruining my movie!" the man hollered into his megaphone.

Phoebe stumbled back in relief, Cole catching her. Piper saw that Paige looked a little unsteady on her feet, too, possibly from the shot that had grazed her temple. She took her sister's arm.

"Just a movie, thank goodness," Phoebe said. "For a second I thought we'd landed in World War Two or something."

"They're harmless," another guy called, coming into view from behind the actors playing Allied soldiers. He carried a large camera, which two other men rushed up to help him dismount from his shoulder. All three were young, tanned, and dressed strangely, just like megaphone guy. White shirts, checkered or striped vests, little white hats that looked made for golfing . . . weird.

"I wonder if they're all doubling as extras," Phoebe muttered.

Piper shrugged. "This does have 'low-budget' written all over it."

Ahead, megaphone guy cursed into the breeze as he tossed his mouthpiece into the sand and stomped off like he was having a tantrum. "Fine! Don't we have any security on this shoot?"

A couple of Nazi soldiers stomped by. "I'll tell ya, I hate wearin' these outfits."

"Yeah, well, the budget's so low on this, you'll be in Uncle Sam fatigues shooting at Jerry's for the reverse-angle shots so it'll look like there's more a' our guys."

An actor looked to the newcomers and pointed past the sandy rises. "Boardwalk's that way. If I were you, I'd be gone before our own tin dictator gets back."

The Charmed Ones and Cole took his advice and crossed the beach to the boardwalk area. Looking back, they saw the whole film crew milling about while the little guy who must have been the director chewed out a couple of big guys in old-fashioned police uniforms.

The boardwalk was a lot quieter than expected. There were no video game arcades and no people talking on their cell phones. There was an outdoor roller-skating rink where mostly women and children were skating. Phoebe was surprised to see that not one woman was wearing pants or even shorts at the beach. And *everyone* was dressed funny.

Many women wore ballet slippers instead of regular shoes. Very old-fashioned versions of "popover" dresses were seen on the female beachgoers, though the unstructured, waistless wraparounds were oddly accompanied by hoods or scarves. A balloon vendor dressed in a white linen suit and a straw hat walked by, making Phoebe wonder who on earth came to the beach wearing a *suit*?

A trio of muscle men hefted barbells on a small stage as other guys walked by wearing short-rimmed, roomy cloth caps. One of the guys sported a pair of white shorts with green and blue polka dots and high white socks. He looked like a color-blind giraffe! Panama hats and safari shirts were also popular.

Despite how oddly everyone else was dressed, it was the Charmed Ones who drew sidelong glances, whispers, and even politely disguised snickers and openly delivered giggles, presumably for the way *they* were dressed. *Weird!*

Phoebe thought. She could understand people looking at Piper, still dressed for the P3 theme night, but the fact was that Piper looked the most appropriate of them all!

The Charmed Ones and Cole walked over to a small shack near the roller-skating rink, where a woman was dressed in a referee outfit and an older guy who might have been her husband leaned against an enormous owl-faced radio. Phoebe had seen one like it in an antique shop once. What was it doing here?

The radio crackled to life. "And here, live in our studio to talk up his film *Yankee Doodle Dandy*, is the great James Cagney!"

A round of applause burst from the radio.

"It's great to be here," a thin, familiar voice said. "Listen, a lot of people think of me as a tough guy. And right now, the world is a tough place. But there are ways to make things not so tough, especially for our boys in the service. We can all do our part, everyday folks can be heroes, too, especially when they buy war bonds!"

"Hear, hear, Jimmy . . . uh, may I call you Jimmy? I wouldn't want to get you mad."

Peals of laughter came from the radio.

"The only thing that gets me mad is people who don't do the right thing. So buy war bonds, today!"

"Spoken like a true-blue Yankee doodle dandy! Next up, an address from President Roosevelt concerning new developments about the war effort in the Pacific."

Cole looked at the others. "I'd say we've come a long way, ladies."

A woman came by handing out flyers for an event to sell war bonds. They each took one, looking at the year printed on the flyer with distress that gave way to alarm.

"Time travel," Paige said woozily. "Again."

"That was a pretty big bang back there," Cole said.

Phoebe jammed her flyer at her ex-husband. "But why are we here? In 1942? What'd you do?"

"Me?" Cole shook his head. "*Leo.* That's my best guess. He kept saying to get the three of you somewhere safe. Maybe this is the last place he felt really safe himself, before he was . . . before what happened to him in combat."

"Fine," Piper said, gesturing at Cole. "Okay, Mr. All-Powerful. Get us back home."

A long, low shudder passed through Cole's tall, impressive form. "That's just it. I've been trying to reopen the portal that took us here ever since we arrived. Nothing's happening."

Phoebe frowned. "So try something else. See how well your powers are working."

"The ones you don't want me to use?" He raised an eyebrow. Phoebe's only answer was an unamused look.

Cole looked around to make sure no one was

watching, then gestured at a small collection of clear soda bottles that had been left on the edge of the boardwalk, standing sentinel over the nearby sand. He waited, and nothing happened. Flicking his wrist, he delivered a series of arcane gestures, but delivered no results.

"What are you trying to do, exactly?" Piper asked.

Cole shook his head. "I tried exploding one of them. That didn't work. Then I just tried moving them, or tipping them over, anything. I can't understand this."

"Bottle," Paige said weakly, holding out her open hand. The glass bottle closest to the front shimmered with blue-white light, vanished, and reappeared in her hand. She passed the bottle to Cole. "Here ya go."

"So *we're* not powerless," Phoebe said. "That's good to know."

"Hey!" Cole snarled defensively. "No one said I was powerless."

"Didn't have to," Piper chimed in.

Suddenly a young boy pedaling on his bicycle with frantic speed tore around the left-hand side of the former attorney and demon. Surprised at how close the boy had come, Cole spun, his barely scuffed shoes slipping on the sand-swept boardwalk. Arms flailing, he fell back, ending up on his side as he hit one of the boardwalk's hot, splintery wood planks, grunting as the edge of a jutting nail scratched his face.

Cole sat up quickly, rubbing at the side of his face. "Now, that's embarrassing." Then he lowered his hand and stared in shock at the crimson streak on his palm. "I'm . . . I'm *bleeding*."

Phoebe stared in amazement. After his return from the demonic wasteland, Cole had been majestic and indestructible. Then, his blood burned through anything it touched, like acid. Now he sat on his butt in a wrinkled, dusty suit, in an undignified pose, looking like a child wearing an incredulous expression. He reminded her of a kid who had just fallen and gotten a scrape for the first time in his life and just couldn't comprehend how this could happen to him.

It almost made her want to lower her guard and feel for him.

Almost.

"Phoebe, my powers are gone," Cole said, his shock giving way to a surprising burst of laughter.

"You mean the ones you picked up in the demon dimension?" Phoebe asked warily.

"Yeah," he assured her, reasoning it out in his own mind before speaking. He nodded, then added, "The timeline isn't going to allow there to be *two* Cole Turners running around in this era. I'm back in my old body!"

Piper tensed. "So you're Belthazor again? And you have *his* powers?"

"You're half right." Cole shook his head. "Just my bad luck that I'd be sent back to 1942. This was when Belthazor was also stripped of powers."

"You've never mentioned this before," Phoebe observed.

He shrugged and said, "It's not something I really wanted to talk about. I still don't. All that matters is that I can't change into his demonic form and I can't use his powers, because, in this era, he didn't have them." Cole gestured at his human appearance. "He was stuck looking like this."

"But Belthazor got his powers back," Phoebe added. "When was that?"

"1943. And I really don't see the necessity of going into the details of how it happened. That won't help us now."

Phoebe appeared satisfied with this explanation, and so she turned to her half sister. "Paige, can *you* get us back?"

"I doubt if I could orb us to that bus stop a block away," she complained. "I'm pretty drained."

Cole jumped in front of Phoebe. "Hey! It's not like I'm completely useless. I lived during this time. I know my way around. And we're all in this together, right? I mean, whether any of us likes it or not, that's how it is. We all want to go home."

"So you want a truce?" Piper asked briskly. "Not that we're formally at war with you or whatever, even if you *have* tried to kill all of us so many times I lost count—"

"That was when I was evil," Cole said quickly. He scratched the back of his neck. "And after I was good and went evil again and went back to good and . . . well, I'm good now, and that's what matters!"

"So . . . a truce?" Piper repeated. "Is that what you're suggesting?"

"Well, yes," Cole said guilelessly. "I think that's in all our best interests."

Phoebe shrugged, turning from her ex-husband. She whispered, "Fine. A truce. But it was *still* fun seeing you fall on your butt."

They walked to the bus stop. The vehicle idling there was an old-fashioned Greyhound, the door still wide open. Above the front windshield, a roll-over sign changed from HERMOSA BEACH to LOS ANGELES.

"Oh, great. L.A. What did we do to end up in L.A.?" Piper said, still brushing sand out of her outfit. "It must have been something really bad."

Phoebe smiled at her sister's dislike of the City of Angels in any era. She fished a five-dollar bill from her pocket, climbed up to the driver, and handed it to him.

He studied the bill, then mashed it back into Phoebe's hand. "What's going on, ladies? You think I was born yesterday? This isn't real. It's play money!"

"But—"

"Off the bus. Now!"

Phoebe leaped back. The driver was about to shut the doors in their faces when Cole surged forward, reaching into his jacket pocket and drawing out a coin that he handed to the driver. "Will this do?"

The driver examined the coin and nodded. "Yep, that'll do fine for the four of you, and here's your change, one shiny nickel."

"I know, don't spend it all in one place," Cole said sourly, taking the coin.

The bus driver's brow furrowed in confusion. "Well, Jack, that's up to you, now isn't it?"

They boarded the bus, taking seats all in one row near the back. The bus soon pulled away, heading into the city.

"What was that all about?" Phoebe asked.

"The thing about the nickel?" Cole shrugged. "I was remembering what things cost in this era, that's all. Penny arcades, Pepsi at five cents a bottle, a quart of motor oil for twelve cents, seven cents for nail polish remover—"

Even Paige managed to rouse herself long enough to give Cole a strange look over that last one.

"So I was told," Cole said sheepishly.

"Yeah, yeah, yeah," Phoebe groused. "Enough memory lane. We need to get back to the twenty-first century."

"Phoebe, cut it out," Piper demanded. "Cole's human and defenseless. I hate to even think about it, but, the way things are now, *he* could be an innocent we have to protect."

"Cole? Innocent?" Phoebe smirked. "That'll be the day."

"She does have a point," Cole added supportively. "But you have to admit, this truce thing is already working out. I told you I'd come in handy!"

"You've been awfully lucky lately, haven't you, Cole?" Phoebe pressed.

"How do you figure?" Cole wondered.

"The coffee incident, and showing up to be our hero," Phoebe said.

"Getting stuck in 1942," Cole continued sarcastically. "Now *that's* really lucky."

Phoebe huffed and turned away from him. She couldn't help but feel he was behind all of this somehow, no matter what anyone said or did. He would stop at nothing to get her back, maybe even time travel. Although, she had no idea how he pulled it off or what he thought he'd accomplish.

They entered the city, each marveling over how clear the skies were in comparison to their own time. There were fewer cars on the road than any of the witches would have expected, and those that sauntered by had odd shapes, at least by their standards: Their roofs were rounded, often reaching back in a curved arc all the way to the back bumper; rear-tire openings were covered by molded metal; the front grills looked like wide angry fish faces, with glaring headlights, shouting grills, huge rounded front and rear bumpers, and hoods shaped in high, thrusting Vs that narrowed to thin, bulletlike noses and dropped downward, metal trim accenting the dynamic, jetlike flourishes.

Car ads inside the bus hawked brand-new Studebakers, Packard Clippers, DeSotos, and more familiar names like Mercury and Lincoln.

The bus lazily cruised down Sunset Boulevard, the driver calling out, "Passing Sunset and Crescent Heights."

"Hey, there's the Villa Nova," Cole said, perking up a little a few moments later. "And across the street, the Garden of Allah. That's like the Viper Room of this time."

Soon they were going by large hotels like the Chateau Marmont and the Sunset Towers, a thirteen-story art deco tower adorned with mythological creatures, zeppelins, airplanes, and Adam and Eve.

Cole snickered as he nodded at the Towers. "They kicked Bugsy Siegel out of there for placing bets at the hotel. That guy never did have a lot of brains."

"Thank you, Tour Guide Cole," Phoebe said, her voice dripping with sarcasm. She wasn't happy to allow him to be their leader, but he was the only one remotely familiar with the city—and the decade.

"Ah, there!" Cole leaned over Phoebe and pulled the wire indicating he wanted to stop. "This is our stop."

The Charmed Ones followed Cole off the bus,

and as it pulled away, he pointed at a pawn shop across the street.

"Uh-huh," Phoebe said questioningly.

Cole spread his hands amicably. "Listen, I don't know why we're here or how long it's going to take us to find a way back. What I do know is that, in the meantime, we're going to need cash. You girls are still wearing some jewelry. It's bound to be worth something."

Piper's shoulders slumped. "He's right."

"You wait here," Phoebe commanded.

Cole saluted. "You bet."

The Charmed Ones left him leaning against a telephone pole. Entering the pawn shop, they were startled by the strange items strewn about. Phoebe noted a toaster the size of a microwave oven, an RCA Victor radio that was only missing the cute little dog with his head cocked to one side, and odd little wristwatches with khaki bands, the sign above them advertising "the Mido Multifort Super Automatic Wristwatch, stainless steel case with radium numbers, radium-filled blued steel hands, brushed silver dial. Early style automatic with bumper rotor winds only with action of moving wrist, not manually."

Piper stared at the watches, wondering if Leo had worn one. Was he a sucker for gadgets then? Always wanting the latest model of everything? Or was he much like her Leo? Traditional, down-to-earth (when he wasn't "up there"). She realized that what she thought of as traditional might just have been Leo's desire to keep something of his past life alive in his present one.

A round-bellied old man in a tight-fitting suit wandered in from the back, starting as he saw the revealing outfits of two of the three sisters.

"Goodness, me!" the man behind the counter bellowed, taking them in. "Did you just come in off the beach and forget to get dressed or something?"

Piper stammered, "We, uh, er . . . their clothes were stolen."

"Ah." The pawnshop owner smiled.

Phoebe chimed in. "Along with everything else. Our handbags, money—"

Now the old guy appeared concerned. "Been to the police station, have you?"

Paige drew a sharp breath and pulled herself together long enough to say, "There's nothing they could do to help."

Phoebe nodded vigorously. "Yeah, they said it happens all the time."

"That's a shame." The portly man frowned. "See you still have some jewelry."

"Thank goodness."

"Don't think I'll ever understand fashion. But this time, it may have saved your bacon. Whatcha got there?"

Piper had an Italian gold bracelet, Paige a pair

of eighteen-karat-gold earrings. Phoebe reluctantly parted with a silver chain with a small diamond pendant.

Minutes later they were back across the street, Piper once again counting their money as Phoebe grabbed Cole. "You were talking about the hotels back there. Which is the best?"

They walked back on Sunset toward the spots Cole had mentioned earlier, which were only a few blocks away. "The Towers is more glamorous, but the Marmont is better for privacy, discretion. Why?"

"I say we go with glamour," Paige said, holding her head, which was now throbbing.

They walked for another block and a half, the "glamorous" hotel Cole had mentioned quickly coming into view. They stopped when they were directly before it.

They entered the spacious, well-appointed lobby, already prepared for the odd looks they would encounter.

No one gave them a second glance.

"This place is for the semirich and the semifamous," Cole informed them. "They're used to eccentrics."

Phoebe and Cole helped Paige onto a couch in the foyer's resting area, a dozen feet off from the concierge's station. Piper went to secure a couple of rooms.

Moments later Piper came back, shaken and stirred. She gave her sisters the bad news.

"They want *how much* for a room?" Phoebe asked.

"More than we've got," Piper said ruefully. "I have the feeling the only thing we're going to be able to afford is some flophouse, or fleabag hotel."

Cole saw his chance and took it. "There's no reason for it to come to that."

"What do you mean?" Piper asked suspiciously.

"There are *plenty* of other ways to get money." Cole's sudden smile was devilish in the extreme.

Phoebe drew back from him. "What do you have in mind?"

"Nothing bad. Nothing illegal." He hesitated, withering somewhat under Phoebe's intense and silent glare. "Okay, kind of bad, kind of illegal, but there wouldn't be any innocents involved, believe me."

"Nothing doing—," Phoebe started.

Piper cut her off. "We're listening."

The former demon smiled. "Thank you. Okay, it's simple. Out of the four of us, I know the most about this era. In fact, I have a lot of highly specific information about all kinds of goings on with criminals and demons at this exact time and place.

Piper was wary. "Cole, what are you suggesting?"

"I still have all of Belthazor's memories; I can't forget things, even if I want to. It's just part of who and what I am." Cole looked away, his shoulders tight, his muscular body tense, as if he were laboring under a terrible weight of conscience. "What I can do is use some of this information to get us some real cash. There's a crime boss on the west side who would pay big money to find out which of his lieutenants has sticky fingers and has been stealing from him to fund his own little criminal activities. And there's another on the east side who would be pretty interested to know the name of the pretty boy his moll has been stepping out with behind his back."

"Okay," Piper said, considering this. "But are they supposed to find these things out? I mean, like now, or ever?"

"I wouldn't do anything to disrupt history," Cole assured her. "The two items I mentioned, and a handful of others I can come up with, are all things that are meant to become known right around this time. It may be that all along I was the one who put the right word in the right ear for the right amount of cash, and if I *don't* go and make some money as a stoolie, then the timeline will be changed anyway."

"I don't trust him," Phoebe said warily.

Piper frowned. "No kidding. And just because we've called a truce doesn't mean any of us should turn our backs on him for a second if we don't have to. At the same time, we shouldn't be letting our feelings get in the way. We should just be careful, all right?"

Phoebe grudgingly nodded. "All right."

Piper went on, "This sounds like our best bet for making some quick cash, and Cole may be right, this could be the way things were meant to happen."

"I think we should let him try," Paige said, weakly stirring. "He may be right, and just 'cause he's evil doesn't make him all bad." A look of utter confusion overtook the fiery-haired witch. "Oh, you know what I mean."

"Fine," Phoebe said. She aimed a wary but determined look at her ex. "Paige should see a doctor, and we need to look less 2004 if we're gonna be walking around trying to find a way home. The money we have won't buy much. So go. Shake down some demons."

Sighing, Cole left the ladies in the foyer. The bellhop chatted them up several times, and one of the assistant managers spoke kindly to them, yet it was clear that the hotel employees were wanting to know the intentions of the three young women.

"Our Bentley broke down on the beach," Phoebe vamped in a haughty voice, trying to buy them some time. "We had to take a common taxi here. Even worse, that scoundrel of a cab driver took off with all our belongings."

"The police!" the pear-shaped, walrus-looking assistant manager cried in alarm. "We must call the police."

"No, no," Phoebe said, waving her hand in dismissal. "Police are so . . . tacky. Our chauffeur is walking back to the estate. He'll pick up the spare Rolls and some pocket change and we'll be good as new."

Piper looked at her sister like she was crazy, but they seemed to be buying it.

"We'll just rest here if it's all right with you," Paige piped in.

The hotel staff was more than pleased to accommodate the three beautiful women for a while. The assistant manager smiled and said, "As you wish."

Phoebe looked at the clock, wondering how long it would take Cole to return . . . or if he would even bother to come back at all. The moment he found himself around great evil, he had a tendency to get drawn right in to all manner of bad business.

She didn't want to be right with her negative feelings about Cole. It was just that after all they had been through, it was so very hard for her to trust him, even with something like this.

She watched the clock—and hoped Cole would be back soon.

Two hours had passed when Cole reentered the lobby.

"Ladies, we're rich," he announced. His plan had gone off effortlessly. He showed them the two hundred dollars and change he had secured.

"Wonderful," Phoebe said, helping Paige up off the couch and steering her toward the check-in counter, trailing just behind Piper and Cole. "One problem down, two or three hundred thousand left to go."

"Hey, look on the bright side," Cole said, glancing over his impressive shoulder. "At least we're together!"

That much Phoebe knew all too well. It seemed that no matter what she did, no matter where she might go, Cole Turner would always be a part of her life.

For worse . . . or for better.

Chapter

5

Later that afternoon, after settling into their rooms, having a quick bite in the hotel's restaurant, then making a brief foray to a nearby department store to buy some more-suitable clothing, Piper and Phoebe met in the lobby, where Cole was once again pouring through newspapers and magazines. Phoebe couldn't help but notice the change in Cole. It was apparent even in the way he stood and held himself. He was having to exert great effort to maintain his confident—even arrogant—veneer. She had seen him completely human only once before, for a short time after Belthazor, his demon half, had been drawn out of him and vanquished, and before he was given the power that made him the Source. During that time, he had been half out of his mind as he desperately searched for the means to help protect the Charmed Ones, or to regain what he had lost.

Now, looking at him as he did everything he could to seem like the same Cole Turner he had been in the present, Phoebe wondered if he could really be trusted to help them any further, or if, truce or no truce, they should tie him up and lock him in a closet until they found a way home.

"Ready?" Phoebe asked her sister.

Piper drew a deep breath and let it out slowly. "As ready as I'll ever be. Paige will be resting awhile. The hotel doc said he'd check on her every half hour."

"Good."

They headed for the door, Cole hurrying ahead of them to open it, but the bellhop beat him to it. All three headed to the street, Cole calling over to them, "Hey, ladies, I'm kind of going your way. Mind if I tag along?"

Phoebe *did* mind, but she held her tongue and grunted in acquiescence. While it was true that Cole had been performing a useful service by going through those newspapers and magazines and becoming familiar with all the little details of this era once more, he didn't have to choose this moment to leave the hotel. He had been waiting for her, she was certain of that, and now he was following her. Watching her.

Just as he had been in their time.

Phoebe took the lead, determined not to let Cole's behavior upset her. She strutted along in her blue knee-length dress, which sported widely spaced plaid checks and large shoulder pads, and was complemented by a red belt and low-heeled red shoes. Piper wore a simple white dress with thin blue stripes, large shoulder pads, a blue belt, and white shoes. She also wore a small blue felt hat that made her feel like her *gram's* gram, for heaven's sake. But that was the style.

The period garb was a fun change from their usual demon-fighting modern clothes, but the sisters found a new appreciation for the advancements lingerie had made over the years. Underneath their clothes they each felt the tug of a "waspie"—a corset that defined the waist and lifted the bustline. Catching up to her sister, Piper wouldn't stop complaining about how restricting the undergarments were to her movements. She felt like the mummy from that old horror film. Phoebe thought they were kind of sexy. They had learned, to their relief, that no one wore hosiery because silk and nylon were so rare during wartime.

A cool breeze rushed up against them, and the sky was blue, free of the gathering storm clouds that threatened to unleash a downpour along the beach. The amber afternoon sunlight had become a harsh glare outlining every detail of this strange time, making it all the more real by setting it in such stark focus. The Charmed Ones had traveled in time before, and each journey had threatened, at some point or another, to seem dreamlike, impossible, and unreal. It was the mundane details like the smell of a man's aftershave, the itchy feel of alien and unusual clothing, or even the buzz of a low-flying bee that brought it all home to the travelers: This was real, and any actions they took might have consequences.

For example, just stopping and flirting with some cute guy might make him late to a meeting he otherwise would have gotten to on time. Being late, he might act flustered, never quite recover his composure, and ultimately fail to make a sale he would have if all had remained as it should have been. That one sale could have led to more opportunities and one day made him rich, and the money he would donate to a charity would save countless lives. All gone as a result of the littlest bit of tampering with the natural flow of events.

Of course, if the balance of time was *really* that delicate, then the best thing they could do was hide themselves away in caves until they were old and gray, never speaking to another soul, never doing a blessed thing to try and correct their situation. No, Piper had to believe that while her theory of messing around with the flow of time was indeed correct, that time itself had a way of bouncing back, of finding a course to make everything come out the way it should have from the beginning. It was probably only major events, like accidentally running over a future presidential hopeful while he was on his paper route, that they had to worry about.

Otherwise, how could they do what they needed to in order to find out why they were here and how they would get back?

Piper grabbed her sister's arm in an attempt to get her to focus on the task at hand instead of the odd sight of so many handsome men tipping their hats each time they drew close. Behind them, Cole jealously groused and muttered.

"Now, remember," Piper reminded her, "this place is weird, and people do act funny, at least by our standards, which can be distracting. But Job One is getting home. We need to find other witches."

Phoebe delivered a single sharp nod. "Or anyone with a real interest in magic."

"Right now, I'm not picky."

Frowning, Phoebe added, "I just don't see why we need to get *jobs* if we have enough money and don't need to work. Our job is finding our way home."

Piper leaned in close to her sister and whispered, "Well, for one thing, do you *want* to be dependent on Cole for your every last dime?"

"Good point," Phoebe said soberly.

"And for another, I don't see any ruby red slippers that are going to take us home by just clicking our heels. So we need to interact with these people, we have to find out why we were brought to this place, to this time, and we need to find people who can help get us home."

Cars eased past at speeds that would have seemed a crawl in modern-day California, while they scanned storefront windows looking for Help Wanted signs. Phoebe grew increasingly more vexed, crossing her hands over her chest as she looked at various wares through the windows.

"Okay, give me the short version," Piper relented. "What's bugging you now?"

Phoebe's eyes lit up. "What's bugging me? I'll tell you what's bugging me." She was silent for a few seconds. "There are so many things, I don't know where to start," she said. Then she took a deep breath. "But they don't really matter as long as we can get back to our lives soon. I've got a deadline."

"Yeah, and I've got a husband," Piper said. "Somewhere in 2004."

"Actually, you probably have him here, too," Cole offered. "Somewhere in 1942. Only he's not your husband yet."

"If you're trying to make things better, you're not," Piper answered.

Phoebe gave Cole a pat on the back. "Demons and lawyers. Neither one particularly known for their tact. You can't help it, can you, Cole?"

Cole started to protest. He thought he was being kind. Piper said it didn't matter as long as they stuck to their goal. But Phoebe and Cole continued to bicker.

Suddenly a man in a business suit carrying a

briefcase stepped in front of them. "Ma'am, is this man bothering you?"

Cole snickered. "I don't believe this."

The man's gaze was intense as he eyeballed Cole with unrestrained fury.

Sheesh! Piper realized. *These two could actually get into a fight over this.*

"You know what?" Cole asked, throwing up his hands in mock surrender as he nodded in the direction of the cross street. "I'm going this way anyhow. I'll see you later!"

Cole strutted off, waving at the businessman.

"Ma'am, do you want me to take care of that for you?" the guy with the briefcase asked.

Phoebe looked at the man in surprise. "Well, that's very kind of you. And tempting as it is to take you up on that offer, I'd have to say no." She raised her voice so that it would carry in Cole's direction. "It's not like he's *dangerous* or *powerful* or anything!"

Cole shot a look back over his shoulder, a "fine, whatever," sneer creasing his handsome face before he looked ahead once more and tensed in surprise. He only barely leaped back from the path of an irate cab driver who shook a fist at him and hollered, "Watch where you're going, you joker!"

Clearly startled, the reformed demon looked around nervously for any more traffic and rushed across to the sidewalk, where he quickly lost himself in a crowd. The businessman tipped his hat and went on as if nothing had happened.

"Y'know, after all I've been through, it *is* kind of fun seeing Cole like this," Phoebe admitted as they walked on.

Then Phoebe noticed that Piper was fuming but not saying anything. Not yet. She loved to simmer until she exploded.

Or was asked to explode.

"Okay, turnaround's fair play; what's up with you?" Phoebe asked. She sighed. "Besides the fact that I'm having a hard time with this 'truce with Cole' stuff. Sorry about that. I know it doesn't seem like it, but I am trying. It's just that every time I give him even the slightest bit of ground, he gets all smug and cocky or obnoxious or—"

"I think it's his pride," Piper said. "His pride's wounded and this is his way of dealing with it."

Phoebe considered that perhaps Piper was right. A moment ago Phoebe had been saying how she *gave* Cole some ground. But what did that mean, exactly? Was she saying that she was magnanimously handing out something remotely approaching the kind of civility she might extend to a total stranger?

Piper was right; it had to rankle him. Phoebe said that she'd been trying. She would just have to try harder.

But she still wouldn't *trust* Cole.

"Actually, I'm thinking about that other guy," Piper hissed. "The one who went after Cole."

Phoebe beamed. "Oh, Lancelot or Galahad or whoever?"

"Yes. I'm used to fighting my own battles, thank you," Piper said. "And you should be too!"

"Well, like you keep telling me, look around. This is a different era. Check it out!"

Piper took a good look. She saw men holding doors for ladies, others smiling and taking their hats off whenever they approached a woman. At a sidewalk café, Piper saw a man pull out a chair for a member of the opposite sex.

"Okay, good manners are appreciated. But I can stand up for myself," Piper said stiffly.

"I know that and you know that. And we both know that you could probably kick more butt than Mr. Briefcase," Phoebe said. "But we've got to start fitting in around here, right? That's what you said. So we'll let guys act a little more like gentlemen. You don't mind when Leo does those things for you."

"True. And now I see why he's always doing them. It was a part of the world as he learned it. Phoebe, what do you think is happening to him back there? Does he need my help? Does he need me? I want to go home."

Phoebe took her arm and gave it a loving squeeze. "We will, sweetie. Don't worry, we will."

They walked on in silence, at least for all of a minute or two.

"There's another thing," Phoebe said, nodding at a group of women gathered outside a dress shop up ahead.

"What's that?"

"No green. Except for those guys who were filming back there on the beach, y'know, the army fatigue costumes, there is absolutely, positively no green anywhere in this place. No green dresses. No green hats or handbags. Even labels on products and stuff, there's just no green. What, did they ration green?"

"Actually, yeah," Piper said.

"Get out of here!"

"No, it's true. Leo told me. The army needed as much green dye as possible for uniforms, so they pretty much just put a lock on it. Bought it all up."

"You know, I think we're very lucky to have been born in our era," Phoebe mused, learning a history lesson she never thought she'd have needed.

They strolled to the dress shop window as the bevy of young ladies moved off, an official notice from the government set just inside the glass display.

Phoebe bent low and read a few lines. "Huh. According to this, there's this War Production Board, and their deal is that as much cloth and metal as possible go to the war effort. So that's why the slimmer dresses and shorter skirts . . . um, comparatively speaking."

Both women had found it strange to have their movements limited by the over-the-knee skirts.

A few men walked by and Phoebe studied their clothing. No suit vests at all. Elbow pads were no longer on jackets. Pants didn't have cuffs. More of "everyone doing their part," she figured.

Phoebe stopped, checking her hair in a store window.

"Will you cut it out?" Piper asked, grabbing her sister by the wrist. "You look fine!"

They came to a spot that made Piper beam. Phoebe didn't get it. The place looked like any old drug store.

"This is Schwab's Drugstore," Piper said excitedly. "Leo talked about this place all the time. It's one of those hangouts where celebrities and struggling actors and writers and musicians all came to hang out, and, if they were really struggling, get a free meal. People got discovered here."

Phoebe pointed at a sign advertising a need for kitchen help. "And they're hiring!"

"Even better," Piper said. "I've actually missed being a chef. There's something really exciting about the hustle and bustle of a busy kitchen."

"Whatever," Phoebe said.

"Zip it and smile," Piper said, dragging Phoebe inside and quickly depositing her at a small empty booth near the soda fountain. She hurried toward the swinging doors leading into the kitchen, knocked, and slid inside.

Phoebe looked for a menu, found none, and was about to study the specials listed on the blackboard behind the counter when a pair of ladies a few tables down caught her eye. Their makeup was so caked on it was scary. Yet they were clearly dressed for a hard day's labor at some factory.

Weird.

"I love those Rosie the Riveter shorts," the closest of the women said animatedly. "Of course, it's not like I would shirk my duty anyway. With Joe gone to war, the house is so quiet and lonely, especially at night. Getting to take his place on the assembly line makes me feel great, like I'm doing my part!"

Her companion laughed. "Now here's the funny part. They said I needed a high school diploma to work. Like I wouldn't have one anyway!"

"Yeah, and like they really wouldn't have made some kinda arrangements. All they care about is filling those spots with warm bodies. If you can breathe, you can get work."

Well, good, Phoebe thought. *It shouldn't be too hard for me, then.*

Though, factory work? Assembly lines? Hmm. Could be interesting. Or not. Guess there's only one way to find out.

Two more women stood in a nearby aisle, shaking their heads as they surveyed the half-empty shelves. One wore a flowery hat, the other a set of frilly gloves that reached up over her elbows. These ladies weren't working at any factories, that was for sure.

She couldn't help but eavesdrop, just a little.

"For the first time ever, Stanley and I are doing really well. Compared to where we were when we first got married in thirty-seven, we've got money to burn! The problem is, that's about all it's good for, these days. I can understand mark-ups, but this rationing is really getting to me. And no one's making anything, not unless it's for the war effort."

"I know. But you really wouldn't want to see our boys over there going without, would you?"

"No, not for a second." She laughed. "Just because I understand it, and just because I agree with it—"

"Doesn't mean I'm not gonna complain!" both women said in unison, falling into a fit of laughter.

"Ahem!"

Phoebe looked up quickly, startled by the arrival of a woman who perfectly fit the description of a Boxcar Bertha: big, round, old, and mean-looking.

It was her waitress.

"What'll ya have?" Bertha asked.

Phoebe smiled. "I want a mochaccino, double mocha. Extra mocha."

"What's that?"

The question stopped Phoebe in her tracks. She knew she wasn't in her own time. She understood that things were different here, but some items were just a matter of basic survival. How could they *not* exist in 1942? Phoebe just couldn't quite get her mind around it. Not yet, in any case. "Well, it's a kind of coffee."

"Coffee. Got that. How do you want it?"

Phoebe winced inwardly, already anticipating the waitress's reply, but she decided to go for it anyway. "Decaf?"

Gritting her teeth, the waitress lifted her hand and gestured as if she were wiping sweat from her brow. "Not from around here, are you?"

Phoebe shook her head.

Bertha went to the counter and quickly returned with Phoebe's coffee. "Anything else?"

"Not right now, no," Phoebe said. Then she changed her mind. "Actually, some cream and sugar would be nice, thank you."

"Cream I can do, but no sugar. Sorry, toots. We get rationed, too. Come first thing if you want sugar, that's what I tell everybody. Same deal if you're looking to grab some groceries. You're not going to get any red points back if we've already run out."

"Oh," Phoebe said, smiling so broadly she was certain she must have looked like a complete idiot. She had no idea what the woman was talking about. "Okay."

Bertha took off. Phoebe sniffed her coffee, pleased by how strong the aroma proved to be.

There were close to a dozen people in the place, including four guys having a heated discussion over the key points of some story about a boxer and a mobster's moll and calling each other names like "Runyon" and "Fitz." Phoebe didn't pay them a lot of attention. Her gaze was quickly captured by a pendant on a long silver necklace that hung from the slender neck of a petite young brunette. The girl made a point of looking everywhere *but* in Phoebe's direction while she nervously played with the necklace's chain. The afternoon sunlight caressed and framed her pretty, heart-shaped face and cast tiny sparks in her wide, doelike eyes. Her long, naturally curly hair was pulled back and fastened into a neat bun with a silver butterfly-shaped barrette. She tapped the lean fingers of her free hand on the table, barely touching the cheese sandwich in front of her. Her dress was among the prettiest Phoebe had seen; the off-the-shoulder number had started as a simple ivory dress with blanket stitching on the collar, but a lovely floral print had been added and it was enhanced by detailed beading that nearly made her shimmer. Her unusually full lips were set in a pout.

The pendant was similar in ways to the Triquetra on the Book of Shadows back home. Phoebe took her coffee and casually drifted in the young woman's direction. Nearing her table, Phoebe said, "I love that necklace."

"Oh. Thank you." The young woman stopped fiddling with the chain and looked up brightly. "Would you care to join me?"

"Actually, I would." Phoebe sat down, pushing her coffee to one side, then leaned in, grinning. "Maybe it'll put that grumpy waitress in a tailspin, seeing something out of place."

Nodding, the young woman said, "She *is* a character." Boldly she extended her hand. "I'm Chloe."

"Phoebe." The moment their hands touched, Phoebe felt yet another spark of kinship. She grinned. "So are you a local?"

Chloe nodded. "But I heard the waitress say you're not from around here."

"I can't believe it's that obvious," Phoebe said. "My sisters and I just got here from San Francisco today." She had to explain her lack of knowledge of this place somehow. "I'm sorry to be so forward, but that's a beautiful pendant you're wearing."

Chloe's hand closed over the pendant she wore, as if to hide it from view.

"Is it from a local jeweler? There's just so much I need to learn about L.A. Where everything is. The best places for clothes, jewelry, a job . . . food!"

Sitting up at mock attention, Chloe adopted the pose of a confident schoolgirl on her first day of class. "Go ahead. Ask me anything."

Where I come from, it's "Ask Phoebe." But hey, when lost in time . . .

"Okay, so tell me something," Phoebe said in hushed conspiratorial tones. "Those two women with all the makeup, the Rosie the Riveters, what is that?"

"You mean, why do they wear so much make-up to go work at a factory?"

"Yeah."

"The factory owners encourage it. My guess is they work at a munitions plant. The makeup helps to protect their skin from any chemicals that might be in use."

"Huh," Phoebe said. That made sense. "One more. I know you're gonna look at me like I've got two heads or something, but here goes. What are 'red points'?"

"You don't have any ration cards?"

"No," Phoebe said warily. "We lived on a ranch. The local farmers bartered with us for food, and the stores for supplies."

Chloe dug a small booklet out of her handbag. There were tiny tickets inside decorated with tanks, navy aircraft carriers, and more. A handful of little cardboard tokens slipped from the booklet. "When you use a ration and you're supposed to get change, you get these little things. They're called 'red points.'"

"Huh," Phoebe said, wondering how difficult it might prove to simply buy necessities without a booklet like this.

"Hey, listen to this one," Bertha called out, turning up the radio behind the counter. All four guys and several other customers in the dining area looked up at full attention.

"Chalk this one up to sugar rationing," said the radio announcer. "A prowler who had a severe case of the old sweet tooth entered the home of Mrs. Eugene Johnson, 3404 Hollywood Street. He contented himself by eating several pieces of candy. Nothing else was touched, according to police reports."

"You're our muse!" one of the men said, scribbling notes on a scrap of paper.

"And don't forget how pretty I am, neither!" Bertha warned.

All four writers promised they would not.

Phoebe and Chloe laughed. Then, shyly, Chloe slipped the necklace holding her pendant over her head and set it down on the table, brushing both their hands. "Can I admit something to you?"

"Go for it."

"Usually I wear this on the inside. I don't like people seeing it, because, y'know, it's private. But with you . . . I just had this feeling you would understand."

"Different people believe in different things. Nothing wrong with that."

"I wish everyone felt that way."

Phoebe felt a deep sadness threaten to over-come her. Was there any era where witches were not persecuted to some extent or another? Of course, she didn't know if this girl really was a witch.

In her time there were groups of women, and some men, too, she thought of as Wiccan wannabes. People who liked the clothes or the jewelry or the incense or even the recipe books one could find at any New Age shop but didn't really believe in any of this stuff. Their interest was far more social, their weekly gatherings having more to do with dishing about one another's boyfriends or coworkers than any serious study of the truly amazing and healing qualities of the Wiccan craft.

But you get that with anything, Phoebe chided herself. The diehards, the devotees, and the dabblers. Someone once told her about a guy he worked with who was a Civil War reenacter. He would go on forever about those who would show up, wear the costumes, want to be a part of the battles, but, at the same time, expect to have every modern convenience. Their cell phones would forever be going off in the middle of triumphant charges or they would have pizzas delivered when they were pinned down behind enemy lines.

Phoebe's instinct told her that this young lady, even if she didn't possess power herself, would have a certain sympathy for magic and its practitioners. She would have an awareness that, in what most considered mundane, ordinary reality, there were worlds, seen and unseen, existing side by side.

She decided just to go for it.

"I believe in magic," Phoebe said.

Chloe's eyes widened, then whatever tension had been in her drained out, replaced by relief. "I knew it!" The young woman took Phoebe's hands and squeezed excitedly. "I just knew it."

They spoke about Chloe's interest in magic, beginning with the day she herself was saved from some pretty dark forces by someone Phoebe believed must have been a witch. Chloe was not a member of any coven here in Los Angeles, but she was already hard at work tracking down the true practitioners in the area. "I'm from Oregon. I was working doing dinner theater when I got the call about Osiris."

Phoebe blinked twice. Hard. "Osiris? As in the Egyptian god?" She *so* didn't want to be going up against pagan deities right now.

Chloe's smile was radiant. "No, but I could see where you would think that. I'm talking about Osiris Studios. Well, one studio really, and a tiny one. It's just one warehouse and about half of the office building next door. Still, ya know, movies."

"What do you do?"

"I make costumes."

Phoebe grinned. "So that explains the great outfit!"

Chloe blushed. "Thanks. Hey, listen. You might

be luckier than you know. You said your sister's in the back looking for a job here?"

"Yeah, that's right," Phoebe said. "I'm kind of looking too."

"Osiris is hiring."

"Really?"

"It's not a lot of money. It's not really glamorous. Just working with clothes all day."

Phoebe perked up. "Clothes, huh? Oh, honey, you have no idea who you're talking to. I'm a born natural when it comes to clothes."

"As far as everyone there goes, I think they're really nice. Things haven't been going as smoothly as they could have been lately, but it's a good place to work. If you want, we can head over there right now."

They rose just as Piper came barreling out of the back wearing a triumphant smile. "Phoebe, hey, great news. I'm working here, and—you're leaving."

"Piper, Chloe. There may be a job for me in the movies. Congratulations, but I've got to run!" Phoebe said, taking Chloe's arm as the pretty young thing was slipping her necklace back on and hiding the pendant under the collar of her dress. This was no problem so far as Piper was concerned. There had only been one job available at the pharmacy, and, considering their real objective was assimilating into this time and finding witches, it made sense for them to spread out through the city. One look at that pendant Chloe was wearing suggested to Piper that Phoebe was definitely on the right track.

"Uh, nice meeting you!" Chloe said as Phoebe practically hauled Chloe outside.

"Uh-huh," Piper said. Then she turned to find Bertha looming over her.

"They hired you, huh?" Bertha asked.

"Yup. I'm Piper."

"I'm sure you are." Bertha frowned. "Ah, just be grateful for the labor shortage. If you can suck up air, you can land a job these days."

Well, aren't you a charmer, Piper thought. Then she turned and got to work.

An hour later and several blocks away, Phoebe emerged from her own interview. The head costumer at Osiris took very well to Phoebe, offering her the job of wardrobe assistant on the spot. Chloe's recommendation certainly helped, but Phoebe had a sense that the trouble her new friend had hinted about was the main reason it had been such a snap to land this gig.

As Chloe had promised, Osiris was indeed the Little Studio That Could. Or might. The main soundstage at the center of the warehouse was split into four separate—and very tiny—sets. Knock on the left-hand wall of a military office and you'd be heard on the other side in a jail cell. Rap on one of those cell walls and someone who looked like he had come from Nazi Germany might coming running. And if you decided to shout too loudly in this one-quarter space, the family from the Midwest sitting by their radio in the living room would hear. Not that all those actors were on stage at a single time, but the idea was clever.

Boom operators were preparing for a scene as camera operators and their assistants loaded a huge magazine of film into a camera. Above, grips, the lighting technicians, aimed glaring fills down at the area while a woman in a dark sweater frowned and went over the script, doubling for the lead actress. Osiris had lost the regular stand-in that morning for some reason that no one was eager to talk about. A tape measure was brought to the woman's forehead and she looked up, glaring, at a young guy who shrugged and called out a number to the focus puller.

It was a bustle of activity. Some of the offices were in the building next door, which meant a lot of running from one place to the other. The costumes that would be needed for the day's shooting were kept in the studio, and it turned out to be Phoebe's responsibility to keep track of them. Clothing had a tendency to wander off all on its own during these ration-happy times.

Chloe took her to one of the offices upstairs. Phoebe climbed the old wood stairs, reached the landing and the hallway above, and paused to survey the studio's second level.

Three catwalks had been strung across the

vast empty space looking down on the sound-stage. Lighting technicians moved across them, busily adjusting their equipment. The hallway before her stretched down to the far end of the warehouse, bent to the left, and ultimately formed a hollow rectangle of walkways with strong metal guardrails. A handful of offices and dressing rooms waited on the second floor, and Chloe took Phoebe to one where raw materials for costumes were kept. Right next door, seen through an open, adjoining doorway, a good-looking but constantly complaining man was having his slicked-back hair doused with hairspray. He wore an army officer's uniform.

"That's Freddy Booth, our leading man," Chloe whispered. "More like our leading *boy*, the way he whines about everything."

They laughed, and Chloe shut the door on the bothersome actor and took Phoebe to a table where bolts of cloth, bits of silk, vinyl, and more were strewn about in a multicolored mess.

"We use whatever materials are on hand," Chloe explained. "It's remarkable how much you can get away with on camera. I've seen Thermoses turned into spaceships or milk cartons into skyscrapers. Ditto with clothes. Some outfit we put together may look ridiculous to the naked eye, but will look like a million dollars through a camera lens. And now, with all the shortages, being creative is more important than ever. And it's not just here."

"Really?" Phoebe asked, still soaking in the details of this new world.

"Back home, my aunt Lizzie has already taken to making outfits for herself and her two daughters out of feed and flour sacks because that's all they had to work with. There's a lot of that going on. City people don't realize it as much." Chloe went to another table and picked up a necklace that appeared to have been crafted from cubic zirconia. "We can do wonders with Bakelite jewelry. This doesn't look like much here, but on camera, it might as well be from the Tiffany collection."

They gathered up a few items the head costumer wanted, then headed downstairs. The small set that was receiving final dressing for the next shot was the army recruiting office. The female lead walked in and Phoebe couldn't believe her eyes.

What was *Paige* doing here? She had just seen Paige less than an hour ago, and the witch had seemed pretty out of it then. Now, on this soundstage, she stood calm, cool, self-possessed, and . . . getting ready to do a scene in front of the cameras?

"Get out of here, no way," Phoebe whispered. The clothing Paige wore—a tight-fitting army uniform—was wildly different from anything they had bought at the department store. Even her hair was different. It was drawn up and piled into a dark olive drab hat Chloe would later tell her was a "hobby hat," a no-nonsense

short-brimmed number decorated with a bird—
wings extended in a black disk at its center—
that many referred to as "the buzzard," though
it was truly an eagle. Just enough of Paige's hair
flared out and cascaded down to frame her face,
and what was not stuffed in the hat was instead
jammed down the back of her collar.

She wore a dark, double-breasted jacket with
high and wide lapels, a lighter-colored shirt and
tie, a tight belt around her thin waist, and a skirt
that fell, respectably, down past her knees. Her
shoes were army clodhoppers, laced down the
center.

"Oh, I know," Chloe said, sliding up beside
Phoebe and nearly startling her. "Isn't she
grand? That's Penny Day Matthews. She's isn't a
big star, not yet, but she's got that star quality,
that real presence, don't you know."

Phoebe's gaze shifted to the set. Behind the
main desk of what looked like an army recruiting
office was a poster of a woman in an outfit similar
to the film's star. The words beside the woman
read: ARE YOU A GIRL WITH A STAR-SPANGLED HEART?
JOIN THE WOMEN'S ARMY AUXILIARY CORPS NOW! And
beneath it: THOUSANDS OF ARMY JOBS NEED FILLING!
WOMEN'S ARMY AUXILIARY CORPS, UNITED STATES
ARMY.

This wasn't Paige. Of course not, how could it
be? Still, the resemblance was incredible!

Freddy, the bore from above, skipped down
the stairs and took his spot from a stand-in.

"Freddy's here!" he announced. "The merriment can now begin!"

A chorus of groans came from the crew. A small but sweet-looking older man in a gray suit with a walrus mustache went over to Freddy and gave him a bit of last-minute direction. Then the older man stepped away and checked with the key members of his crew to see if all was in readiness.

"That's Oscar Lyons," Chloe explained, holding on to a handful of materials the head costumer had requested while Phoebe cradled the rest. "He owns Osiris Studios. He also produces and directs all the movies."

In minutes it was "Quiet on the set," and "Action" was called.

"It's ridiculous!" the actress who looked exactly like Paige said with terrific emotion. "No one treats us with the respect we deserve."

Freddy, the impassive male costar, merely grunted.

The actress went on. "Just the other night, Linda and I went to a restaurant in our uniforms and you know what we were told? 'It's against our policy to seat women in uniform unescorted.' That's what they said. They made us leave."

"Surely you're exaggerating," her leading man said stiffly. He barely even looked her in the eye. Instead he seemed to be directing his attention over her shoulder, at a small mirror on the wall.

"Oh, Roderick, how can I make you understand?" the actress said, grabbing his arms and shaking him so hard that he'd *have* to look at her. "We'd fight and die in this man's army if we were given a chance. As it is, we're doing our part and the newspapers and magazines run articles saying we're not competent, or we're a bunch of tarts."

"Oh, yes, I saw one of those cartoons about you ladies . . . quite funny, I'll give it that."

She turned from him in frustration, careful to make sure the camera always had at least a full profile. "I thought you, of all people, would be sympathetic. Why do you think I'm doing this?"

"I don't know. Why are you?"

She whirled dramatically. "Because I love you, you silly fool! And more fool I, for thinking you'd even notice."

The lead actor appeared startled. It was the first time he had expressed anything resembling true emotion. He shook his head. "I don't know what to say."

"Say that you love me," the actress pleaded.

He turned to the camera and smiled broadly. "No, honestly, quite embarrassing, I know, but I really *can't* think of what to say. Line?"

"Aghhh!" the actress hollered, throwing her hands up in frustration and storming off. "Why couldn't I have just been given a monkey as my leading man?"

"Honey, I think you were," Phoebe said softly.

Oscar called, "Cut," and went over to speak with the leading lady while Freddy was taken aside to review dialogue with the script supervisor.

"And what is it with this broad, anyway?" the actress hollered, Oscar taking a step back to avoid the worst of the verbal explosions, his expression remaining pleasant as always. "Women are signing up to serve their country, not to get noticed by lunkheads like him!"

A slow round of applause from a single pair of clapping hands sounded. Everyone turned as a hauntingly handsome man in an expensive suit and hat stepped out of the shadows and moved near the cast and crew. A half dozen men who looked far less gentle and refined fanned around him.

Hoo-boy, Phoebe thought, judging from the way Chloe had tensed up. *Why do I get the sense that I'm looking at the source of everyone's trouble around here?*

"That's Ned Hawkins," Chloe whispered to Phoebe.

Phoebe nodded. *Bad news has a name. I'll ask Cole to see if he's got a reputation, too.*

Paige's look-alike crossed her arms over her chest as Ned approached her, the crew parting to let him by.

"You're right," Ned said. "A woman like you shouldn't worry her pretty head about getting noticed by a dope like him. You should be getting noticed by someone like *me.* And, by the way, you are."

The actress tensed. "What do you want?"

"Now, don't be like that. I have it on good

authority that if you started being nicer to me, you might have to change your name from Penny Day to Lucky Day . . . because that's what it would be for both of us, toots."

"Did you *really* just call me 'toots'?"

"I did. It's fun seeing you get riled up, though I'd rather see you get riled up in a different way. Guess a guy's just gotta take what he can get."

"Fine. But you won't be *getting* anything." The actress whirled and stormed off.

He started to go after her, but Oscar interposed himself between the newcomer and the departing starlet-to-be.

"Mr. Hawkins," the smaller man said gruffly.

The new guy smiled. "Ned. Call me Ned. I like everyone I work with to feel like we're family."

"*Mr. Hawkins*," he repeated, "this set is private property. That means it's off limits to anyone who I decide is a disturbing factor."

"Me? Disturbing? Not a chance."

"It was the most polite term I could come up with for a hooligan like you."

Ned threw his head back and laughed. "That's entertainment. I love show business people." His smile vanished. "Now, let's go to your office and talk business."

"I have no business with you."

"Oh, I don't know. I heard Osiris is branching out, going international. That would mean that we have plenty of business."

"Again, I think not."

Phoebe saw Freddy slinking away, hurrying up the stairs to the dressing rooms on the second floor.

"Things haven't been so good here lately," Ned said. "You're losing people right and left. Lots of unlucky things happening—"

Suddenly a yelp came from the stairs. Phoebe whirled in time to see Freddy come flopping down, head over heels, landing hard at the base of the stairs, then sitting up to grab his ankle.

"My leg! My leg!" he howled. A dozen people ran to him.

"See what I mean?" Ned asked. "Now *that's* what I call unlucky. Of course, I have been reading the script and I have a good idea of what happens. You've already shot his action scenes. You can get the rest of his coverage from the waist up . . . provided there aren't any other unlucky incidents like this. That would really be the pits, wouldn't it?"

"It would shut us down."

"It would indeed. So Oscar, let's talk."

Reluctantly Oscar called for a break, and agreed to talk with Ned and his people in the offices next door.

Phoebe glared at Hawkins. Could he be another luck demon? It seemed possible, considering the sandy hair, the gray-blue eyes, and the crazy thing that had just happened to Freddy.

And, if that was true, then there was another reason beyond Cole's theory about Leo to explain their presence in this exact time and place. It could be that the Charmed Ones were needed, and this producer and the people who depended on him were the innocents they were meant to save!

"What is it?" Chloe asked, clearly picking up on Phoebe's alarm.

"Those guys," Phoebe said. "They aren't human."

"Tell me about it."

I almost just did, Phoebe thought. Chloe clearly thought that Phoebe was simply referring to the brutal manner in which Hawkins and his men conducted themselves. Right now, it was better that she believed that Hawkins was just another criminal trying to zero in on the movie business. Better, for her sake, that she not connect him to anything truly demonic. *Unless, of course, she already has, and that's why she was on the lookout for witches.*

Phoebe had a pretty good idea that he was something truly inhuman. In fact, considering what happened to Freddy—and right on cue no less—she would be stunned to learn that he wasn't a demon. It appeared some strange magic had been at work.

One of Hawkins's big lugs came a little too close as he followed his boss and brushed against her arm.

"Just be natural," he said, amused at her annoyance. "Don't worry about it."

Phoebe watched the big guy and the other gangsters carefully as they retreated into the back with Oscar.

Natural? There was nothing natural about this.

Except, maybe, *super*natural.

Only Chloe paid attention as Penny Day Matthews silently slipped away toward the exit at the opposite end of the studio. She grabbed Phoebe and together they cut Penny off just as she was leaving.

"Tell me you're not going too," Chloe pleaded. "We'll find a way to deal with Hawkins, I swear."

"I know you believe that, kid," Penny said, "but the bottom line is that I grew up around guys like Ned. He knows what he wants and he won't take no for an answer. Not with Osiris, not with me. I don't want any more people getting hurt. This job just isn't worth it, not for any of us, Oscar included. My bags are already packed and they've been waiting in my car the last two days. By dinnertime today, I'm going to be heading somewhere no one's going to find me, not for a couple of months, anyway. Because, y'know? I haven't even decided myself where I'm going."

"Please, Penny," Chloe begged. "They'll shut down the movie. Oscar will be ruined!"

"Sorry, kid. I love ya a lot. This was my dream too. But it's over."

The actress turned and left without another

word. Chloe whirled on Phoebe. "What are we going to do? She has to stay or there isn't any movie!"

"Actually, I think she made the right choice," Phoebe said, the wheels already turning in her mind, ideas coming into focus. "And I don't think it's all over for Oscar or this place. In fact, I'd say things are just heating up!"

Chapter
6

That night Phoebe filled her sisters in on what she had seen and heard at the studio.

"So, that's it?" Paige asked, feeling much better, though a little flustered at Phoebe's news. "I have a chance to meet one of my father's ancestors face-to-face and now she's flown the coop?"

"I'd say that's the size of it." Phoebe caressed Paige's hair. "Sorry, hon."

"Sounds like there's some serious trouble over at Osiris," Piper said, folding her arms over her chest. "I got to work the counter quite a bit today, and I heard that this isn't the first bit of bad luck the company's been faced with lately."

"I'm thinking Oscar is our innocent," Phoebe said swiftly. "And maybe we were drawn here to help him. I spoke with Cole, and he said he'd find out everything he could about this Hawkins guy."

"You said he looks kinda like that guy Cole saw when we were fighting the Ugly Brothers back in our own time?" Paige asked.

"Same gray-blue eyes, anyway. And I saw that guy too, back at the *Mirror*. He was with another guy with the same kind of eyes. I think we were set up by them."

"Hmmm," Paige muttered. "You think Osiris is being threatened by the ancestors of the guys who were behind what we went through?"

"It's possible. Ancestors, or . . . well . . . with demons, they could just be really old and still look good. Like Cole."

An urgent pounding came at the door. Phoebe looked at her sisters, then went to the door and opened it.

Cole stumbled in, his face bloodied and bruised. Phoebe went to him without hesitation, grabbing him to keep him from falling. She guided him into a narrow wooden chair and he grunted, winced, and made little noises of pain as he settled in. It sounded like every part of him hurt. Piper and Paige ran to find the first aid kit the hotel doctor had left in their room.

"What happened?" Phoebe demanded. She was angry with herself. Despite how hard she had worked to cut herself off from all feelings for the man, concern for Cole still welled up inside her.

"I went to see some old friends," Cole said, lapsing into a coughing fit that didn't subside until Paige returned with a glass of water and he was able to take a few sips. Piper returned next, opening the first aid kit and dousing cotton swabs with iodine.

"This is gonna hurt," Piper warned.

"Yeah, no problem," Cole said, sliding back and easing his head against the wall. He yelped as she dabbed the cotton swabs on the scratches and cuts covering his face. Phoebe helped her sisters strip off his jacket and shirt, and, when he steadfastly refused to have the hotel doctor called in, bandaged his bruised ribs.

"We'd get kicked out of here if they saw the shape I was in," Cole explained a few minutes later. "And it's not that serious. I may be mortal now, but I know a lot about injuries, big and small."

Yeah, Phoebe thought, *because when you were a demon, you inflicted a whole ton of them, didn't you?*

"Some old friends," Piper said, prompting Cole.

"Right," he whispered, groaning a little as he straightened up in his chair. "All I can say is, those demons *used* to be scared of me. Not anymore, apparently."

"Figured that out when they were beating the crap out of you, huh?" Phoebe asked.

"Pretty much. However, I did get some information before they caught on that I couldn't really wave a hand and roast them over an open flame anymore. Then I overhead a couple of other things when I was getting kicked. A lot."

"There has to be an easier way for us to get information," Phoebe said, surprising even herself with her words of compassion for Cole.

Cole frowned. "I've got to admit, it would be nice to have the Book of Shadows around to find what we're up against, but nine-tenths of the law is legwork, or, in the case of what almost just happened to me, legbreaking, and—"

"I thought 'possession' was nine-tenths of the law," Paige said curiously.

"Yeah, demonic possession," Phoebe quipped, attempting to cover up her lapse in maintaining her emotional distance from Cole.

Cole shook his head. "Common misconception. The bottom line is that I've *got* the bottom line on these guys for you. Want to hear it?"

They helped him to his feet, and Cole slowly put his shirt and jacket back on as he spoke. "So, what this breaks down to is, things are the same wherever you go—or pretty similar, anyway. You've got your human underworld: killers, blackmailers, organized crime, the list goes on. And you've got the demonic underground: spreading the influence of evil, internal power struggles, corrupting or destroying good, yadda yadda. Just as there is in our time, here in 1942 there's overlap. You get demons seeking to achieve their ends using mechanisms put into place by ordinary humans."

"You mean like posing as lawyers," Phoebe said pointedly.

"Hey, I had to pass the bar," Cole said testily. "I didn't just conjure up a certificate to put on the wall."

"*Children . . .* ," Piper warned.

"Right," Cole said contritely. "You get overlap. Human gangsters and demonic overlords forming partnerships because their interests overlap. Sometimes you have humans trying to gain supernatural power, but, more often, it's the other way around. Hawkins and his brood aren't exactly from around here. They come from a particular plane of existence in a demon dimension where their society is very strict. Regimented. So much so, that life becomes extremely predictable. Skip ahead a couple of million years. Now things have gotten to the point where everyone knows exactly what's supposed to be happening at any given time, in any given situation, usually before it's supposed to happen. They've evolved. This power has become a survival mechanism for them."

"So they have a sixth sense," Paige said.

"Yeah. That's part of it. But to be able to compete among themselves, for wealth, power, glory, women, whatever, it's not exactly a level playing field for these demons. Some are a little better at this than others. Some are a *lot* better. The Hawkins brood is particularly good at this stuff, and they can do one other thing. They push things along, exerting a kind of physical influence on people and on events."

"So they cast spells," Piper said.

Cole's face darkened. "What I'm trying to get across to you is that they're *dangerous*. Nine times out of ten, they get whatever it is they want."

"Fine," Phoebe said sharply. "So what do they want now? Why hassle Oscar and Osiris?"

"Good question. All I've been able to put together is that the Hawkinses are into something major. Something a lot bigger than some simple extortion scheme or wanting to have a legitimate business to launder their money through. I heard at least one of the demons talking about 'objects of power,' and the way he spoke, it's not penny-ante stuff that the Hawkinses have their hands on."

"We've dealt with magical doodads before," Phoebe said. "We just have to find out where they are and Piper can blow them up. It's got to be bigger than this."

Cole wasn't going to be turned away from this subject so easily. "People don't want to know this, but there are things out there, not many of them, a couple of swords, a dagger, some nifty amulets and bracelets—jewelry's always a big one, for some reason—these things that, whatever form they're in, can crack open worlds. Affect destiny. I think somehow these guys have gotten their hands on this stuff and themselves into the middle of something big."

"So they need Osiris to do whatever the Big

Nasty is that they're up to, is that it?" Paige asked.

"That would be my guess," Cole said. "What we need is somebody who can get in there, who can get close to Hawkins, and get him to reveal the particulars."

Cole had looked directly at Paige as he said this. Phoebe was looking right along with him. They were finally seeing eye to eye.

"Whoa, whoa, wait a minute," Paige protested. "Me? *I'm* supposed to be the Undercover Sister?"

Piper didn't like the sound of this, either. "You said these guys know all, see all, right?"

"No, it's perfect," Cole said. "Yeah, they have all this power, but they're arrogant. Hawkins either wants so desperately to believe that Penny will fall for him that there's no question in his mind that it'll happen, despite what his instincts are telling him, or he's already got a sense that it will happen so he's not looking that closely at things. And the reason he thinks it'll work between him and Penny is because Paige is going to be there in Penny's spot, playing along. So, in a way, he's right. But, in another way that he won't see, that totally helps us, he's wrong, and that'll make him vulnerable."

Phoebe nodded. "I talked with Chloe already, and she's willing to help."

"I dunno . . . ," Paige moaned.

"There are innocents involved," Phoebe said. "We can't turn our backs on them."

"Fine," Paige said at last.

"How do we explain why I'm not staying at Penny's digs?" Paige asked.

Piper shrugged. "Easy. Just put in an appearance over there now and then."

"I don't have her keys or anything."

"Chloe can help with that. She looked after the place a couple of times when Penny went off to New York for some auditions."

"Okay," Paige said, throwing her arms open wide, "make me a star!"

Everyone at the studio made a big fuss over Paige as she arrived for work the next day. And why not? They thought she was Penny Day Matthews. The resemblance was uncanny. By all accounts, they even sounded identical. Penny had been working with these people for weeks, completing ten of the studio's twenty shooting days allocated for this picture.

She was rushed into hair and makeup, Chloe never once leaving her side. Paige had jitterbugs dancing away inside her. She had two performances to give. The first involved remembering her lines from the screenplay—which really wasn't *that* hard. She had been diligently memorizing spells right and left for months; this dialogue, corny as it was, really wasn't that big a deal, at least in comparison. After all, in front of a movie camera, she could get as many takes as she needed to get a scene right. They could even hold up cue cards!

Spells, though . . . get one word wrong in a mystical battle, and you could end up the vanquishee instead of the vanquisher.

Truly, it was her *other performance* that had her more concerned. Penny had built up relationships with not only her fellow cast members, but also the crew. Paige had no idea who any of these people were. Chloe had done her best to fill Paige in, but the red-haired witch had been loaded with so much information that she just couldn't keep it all straight. She would just have to form her own impressions of these new people and forge all new bonds with them.

Paige's first order of business was seeing to Chloe's promotion to personal assistant. Oscar hadn't objected. So far as he knew, if it hadn't been for Chloe, his star would have stayed away and production would have been over. And that was true, though he didn't really know *all* the particulars. The fewer people who knew about the switch, the better.

So it was Chloe's job, each and every time, to intercede when anyone spoke to Paige, calling her, of course, "Penny."

"Penny, do you have fifteen minutes in your schedule for a sit-down with a reporter from the *Chronicle*?"

"Why, *Roger*," Chloe would jump in, "that's so very exciting! Penny, isn't Roger doing a fabulous job as *publicist*?"

"You really are, Roger!" Paige would say. "Thanks!"

Meanwhile Paige would think frantically, *Roger, Roger, rhymes with codger. No, that's no good. He's young and handsome. . . . Roger Dodger, quick on the uptake, always knows what to say. Maybe . . .*

Or:

"Penny, darling, here are your sides for today!"

"Oh, *Lucy*, you're right on top of things," Chloe would chime in. "We couldn't ask for a better *script supervisor*!"

"Thank you, Lucy!" Paige would say, taking the last-minute rewrites.

Lucy . . . Lucy . . . Lucy Goosey? Lucy in the Sky with Diamonds?

How am I ever gonna remember all these people?

The task grew easier as the day went on. Sometimes her memory tricks served her just fine, as was the case with her costar, Freddy. What an overactor!

Ready Freddy! Who woulda thought you could squeeze that much ego into one five-foot-four frame?

His line deliveries were overwrought. Oven roasted. And he served them up *hot*, always ticked off about some little thing here or there that would go wrong on the set.

Still, he was always ready . . . ready to make some snide comment, ready to complain, ready to chase after her and try to get up her skirt, despite his crutches and the cast on his leg.

There were two big moments of truth for

Paige that day. The first came when she had her first scene, which went a lot better than she would have expected. It was a scene on the "home front" set, with Paige playing a young woman coming home after romping about with her boyfriend and finding her parents stricken, sitting wordlessly next to the big radio. The broadcaster was describing the attack on Pearl Harbor, and informing listeners that the U.S. was officially at war.

Calling up the kind of shock necessary for this scene meant thinking about the day she had woken up in the hospital after the car crash that had taken her parents' lives and realizing she would never, ever have a chance to make things right with them. Or so she thought at the time. Since then, a journey into her own past had helped her to put her old inner demons to rest, though she had been unable to save their lives, try as she might. Time had found a way to keep its flow from being disrupted, and the Angel of Death would not be denied.

Strangely, thinking of such things and allowing herself to feel all those emotions once more proved to be more of a spiritual cleansing than a torturous ordeal, and everyone on the set had been *stunned* at the performance she had given.

The second and more difficult challenge came when Ned arrived on the set just after they had taken the break for lunch.

Evil or no, he really was a hottie, and that

made the job of getting close to him just a little easier.

He regarded her strangely, his tough-guy act falling by the wayside instantly. "You seem different."

Can he tell I'm not Penny? Paige refused to give in to panic. "That's 'cause I've been thinking."

"About what?"

"Us."

He smiled, then, struggling, forced his expression back into neutral. "I didn't realize there was an 'us.'"

She shrugged. "Well, if you're not interested . . ." Turning, she headed off for craft services.

"Whoa, whoa!" Ned said, losing his cool facade completely as he raced around in front of Paige, cutting her off. "I didn't say that. This is just . . . unexpected."

"Didn't expect me to come around this fast, huh?"

"I don't know. *Is* that what's happening?"

Paige felt calmer, more in control of the situation. "Could be. If you play your cards right."

Realization seemed to light in his gray-blue eyes. "Okay. You want to cut some kind of deal."

"You open to that?"

He smiled. "Could be."

"So let's talk terms. I'll go out with you. As in, we will date. Nothing more. Nothing less. I'm not going to be your girlfriend, or your moll, or whatever. When we're out together, you will behave like a gentleman. Get grabby and you'll wish you hadn't. Expect nothing and you will not be disappointed. You will get my company, my attention, and I might even give you a fair chance at changing my very negative view of you. But that's all you get."

"Sounds peachy. What do you get in return?"

"You take it easy on Oscar and Osiris. No more accidents. No more threats. Whatever it is you want, you make your proposal like a businessman, and if he says no, that's it. No repercussions. No reprisals."

Ned grinned. "Are you finished?"

She nodded—and he started laughing!

"What?" she asked, curious and a little annoyed.

"I should have you on my financial investment team," he said. "You're tougher when you're making a deal than Barrish, and he's the guy who made me rich!"

"You two are close," she said, subtly probing for information.

"He's my most trusted advisor. A surrogate father as well."

"And what does dad think of me?" Paige asked.

"He says you're too much trouble, and I shouldn't divide my attention."

"He's right."

"Don't I know it. But some things are just meant to be, I think."

Paige smiled. "We'll have to find out."

Actually, spending time with Ned could help on every conceivable front. It would explain why she would seem different to those who knew Penny, justify if she seemed distracted or worried, if she made mistakes.

Plus, if Cole was right, and these guys trafficked in stolen mystical artifacts, then getting close to Ned would indeed set her on the path to helping them get back to their own time.

Of course, there was the matter of all the lugs who followed him around. They were a pretty uptight bunch, even for demons.

Maybe she could sit 'em all down for a game of I Never. Heh. *That* usually loosened people up.

"So . . . ," Ned began. "Dinner?"

"Yeah, for starters. Pick me up here at eight."

"Already done." Ned turned, his hand lightly brushing hers. Paige felt an almost electric charge pass between them, and worried for the first time that if she didn't watch herself, she just *might* fall under this guy's spell.

Chapter

7

When Paige had accepted Ned's invitation to dinner, she wondered how she might survive the ordeal. Now she was actually finding him quite nice company.

Was it because she sometimes had a fondness for bad boys? Or was it something more?

Ned had taken Paige to Romanoff's on Rodeo Drive. The French cuisine was the finest in the city, and the celebrities who lined up to eat here happily put up with the owner's steady stream of insults and the chuffing bulldogs who ate with him at his table. Groucho Marx sat with Louis B. Mayer at one table, Billy Wilder and Alfred Hitchcock at another. A bronze plaque with the name "Humphrey Bogart" etched into its surface hung above a nearby booth. It turned out that when Bogie wasn't shooting, he came here for lunch every day.

"I love the story behind this place," Ned told her. "Did you read about it in *Life*?"

Paige shook her head.

"Good. I enjoy telling this one. Okay, the guy over there with the bulldogs? He's known as 'Prince Mike.' That's short for Prince Michael Romanoff, cousin to the late czar of Russia."

"Impressive."

"Would be, if it were on the level. The truth is, he's a Lithuanian immigrant named Harry Gerguson. What's terrific is he comes over here with his Old World manners and his Oxford accent, and he decides to pass himself off as royalty. The next thing he knows, he's invited to all the fancy parties, he's playing polo at the biggest matches here, and the studios put him on retainer as technical advisor for anything that's supposed to be set in Russia."

Paige shook her head in amazement. "No one checks up on this guy?"

"Oh, they do. But they like him, see? He's got chutzpah to spare. So everyone just goes along with it. He decided a year ago to open this place, and Jack Warner, Cary Grant, Darryl Zanuck, all these guys, put up the dough. Last month he bought 'em all out."

"And everyone thinks this is a good thing?"

"It's America," he said. "You are what you say you are. And Hollywood . . . this is where dreams come true. It's perfect!"

"So what kind of dreams do you have?" Paige asked.

"I can't tell you that. Banzaf—Barrish," he corrected himself quickly, "he'd have my head!"

Paige caught him studying her, trying to see if she had made anything of his little slip. She lowered her gaze and changed the subject. "All my life, I've just dreamed of making it." She looked at him. "And on my terms. Can you understand that? No one pulling my strings."

"You won't get any argument out of me," he said, the tense moment already past. He seemed satisfied that she hadn't even noticed that other name he had called his advisor. But Paige knew all too well that some demons had "true names," and to know them was to have power over them.

"Did you grow up here?" Paige asked.

"Naw. I grew up in Grosse Point, outside of Chicago. My dad had a club, and I made extra money after the crash in twenty-nine as a caddie and changing the pins at the bowling alley. Did some boxcar jumpin' for a couple of years to see the country, even got myself locked in a refrigerator car once! The thing I always carried with me, though, was that club, and the entertainers who come in. Fatty Arbuckle, all them guys."

Paige smiled. She could hear his Chicago accent come out when he got excited. Otherwise, it seemed he took great pains to cover it up.

"So, what is it you do, exactly?" Paige asked, pouring it on thick with the innocent routine.

Ned flexed his strong fingers, and his lips

quirked into an almost smile. "You should think of me like an architect. Instead of designing buildings, or things like that, I engineer circumstances, possibilities, to create potential. I study probabilities. I make things happen."

He gestured and the lights dimmed. A murmur rose up from the crowd of diners.

"What happened?" Paige asked.

"Don't know. Something must have shorted out. Just the luck, huh? But this is more romantic."

A waiter came by, lighting the candles at their table:

"You bet," Paige agreed.

Charming guy, Paige thought. *I'll give him that.*

That and maybe, *maybe,* a good night kiss.

Eventually.

If she had to.

Yeah, that would be torture, she teased herself.

"So why aren't you acting?" Paige asked. "You're good-looking enough."

She flushed at her own impulsive and leading question. Was this man working some kind of magic on her? Did he have her in his spell? Did she really feel some connection to him?

"I don't have a lick of talent in that department," Ned said with a false modesty that did not become him.

Paige guessed that this man was acting all the time. He'd have to be, to fit so neatly into human society. Her annoyance must have shown because he quickly added, "I've been tempted, but it just wouldn't be smart. I'm a businessman, first and foremost. To succeed, you have to concentrate on one thing and see it through. What is it I read somewhere? Oh, right. 'Be here now.' Give whoever, or whatever, is in front of you your full attention."

He sat comfortably, his hands on the table, lightly clasped, his thumbs always in plain view. Odd.

He caught her staring. "It's something Barrish, my advisor, taught me. If you hide your thumbs, people think you're not trustworthy. Show them, and it makes people relax. I couldn't tell you why."

"It probably has something to do with enemies facing off," Paige said, suddenly aware that she had been clasping her own upper arms, hiding her thumbs. Relaxing, she set her hands palms down on the table. She hadn't come here to fight, after all. She needed to learn more about who and what she and her sisters were up against, trick her enemies into lowering their guard.

"Not something I have to worry about. Most people are pretty transparent to me."

"Huh! Pretty sure of yourself, aren't you?" Paige asked.

Ned's smile was movie-star caliber, no doubt about it. "Most women find confidence to be an attractive trait. What about you?"

Paige playfully angled her head to one side. "I suppose the question you've got to ask yourself is, 'Does she look like most women?'"

He laughed heartily and unabashedly, his icy-calm veneer of self-possession vanishing in a heartbeat. "I like you, Penny. We're gonna have good times, I can see it."

"Can you?" Paige asked, drawing out the words to a purr, managing to sound demure and tempestuous all at once—a trick she worked on in her spare time. This wasn't going to be nearly as tough as she thought it would be. In fact, she would have to watch herself and make sure she didn't start having too good a time. One Charmed One in love with a demon was plenty!

Phoebe changed back into her modern clothes, a luxury in which she could only indulge when she was safely behind the locked door of the room she shared with Piper and Paige. Three to a room meant one of them had to sleep on the floor at night, and lately that had been Paige, considering the late hours she had been keeping on the arm of a demon.

Cole, naturally, had gallantly offered to let Phoebe sleep in his room on his second bunk. "No funny business, I promise" had been his mantra, with "Hey, you've still got powers, you could kick my butt if I tried anything!" thrown in for good measure. Phoebe was altogether certain she could kick Cole's backside with or without powers, but she chose not to engage him in the discussion. It was best to stick to the task at hand so they could get back to their own time and go back to their respective, separate lives. The last thing Phoebe wanted was to get stuck in this time and place, especially with Cole.

A breeze?

Turning, Phoebe realized she had left the window open, the drapes pulled aside. *Oh, great. Now half the neighbors have probably seen me wearing this getup. And, um, getting into this getup.*

A sharp rapping came at her door. Three quick taps. *Tock-tock-tock.*

Phoebe's brow furrowed. That almost sounded like a signal. Three knocks, the Power of Three . . . but she hadn't worked out a signal with her sisters. Piper was working for another hour yet and Paige would only be home this early if something had gone south with her luck-demon Romeo.

She looked down at her outfit, loving—no, *really* loving—the soft feel of her own twenty-first century clothes. She did have a robe to throw over them so as not to draw questions from whoever was knocking.

Piper or Paige had keys. So that left only Cole, or someone from the hotel's staff, maybe.

The rapping came again. It was more insistent this time. Phoebe frowned. What if it was the walruslike Mr. Peters, come to complain about noise or to politely hit them up for more rent in advance?

I don't wanna answer you, Phoebe thought, knowing that if she'd expressed those words she would have sounded about five. *Go away!*

There was only silence from her door.

"Good," Phoebe whispered.

Suddenly a fiery luminescence tattooed itself upon the inner door, searing the words DON'T PANIC into the wood. Then a woman dressed in a billowing black evening dress *melted* through the door, her ink-black bangs rising and falling with the magical energies she controlled. She was stunning—but, then, evil often was.

"Whut-ow!" Phoebe cried, stumbling back and looking for some spot in their already cluttered room that would allow her enough space for a good fight.

The woman's gaze was patient and kind, a stark contrast to her smoldering and sexy appearance. Her wasp-thin waist, towering legs, long, practically Egyptian-looking black hair . . . the whole thing conspired to shout, "Creature of the night!" Yet the woman gave off the aura of a good egg.

Oh, no, I'm using their lingo now!

The intruder opened her hands. "I said, 'Don't panic.' Relax. Chloe sent me. I'm one of the good guys. I'm a witch, like you."

Phoebe relaxed, but only a little. "You're a witch," she repeated softly, tentatively.

The woman laughed. "I've been called worse."

"No, I mean, like . . ." Phoebe was going to say "like me," but she stopped herself.

The woman's amusement was apparent. "I understand your reticence to reveal who and what you are. Though I'm afraid I have revealed your secret to young Chloe. She was close to guessing as it was."

"That I'm a witch?" Phoebe asked, still not fully admitting it.

"You're not just a witch. You have unfathomable powers. My power is great enough that I can sense it clearly. My goal is to help others, so, in that way, we're very much alike. You can trust me, I promise you."

Phoebe nodded, kind of getting into this now. "Well, I've got to say, you do have a cool fashion sense!"

"My name is Theda McFey. I'm an actress. That's my day job, anyway."

"Oh. I'm a columnist."

Theda backed away, raising her hands in mock alarm. "Not like that evil Hedda Hopper, I hope!"

"Hedda who?"

Lowering her hands, Theda said, "She's a gossip columnist. You should have seen her and Joan Fontaine going at it over at the Brown Derby. And right after Fontaine won the Academy Award for best actress, no less. That was for the movie *Suspicion*, by the way, and if you still have one or two of those about me, I quite understand. I've been dubbed 'the vampire' by the local rags and I've found the image helps open doors for me. In fact, I'm leaving tomorrow to begin work on an Egyptian epic in which I'll be playing Cleopatra. No real stretch there. I've had men at my feet all my life."

"I'll bet you have," Phoebe said.

Theda nodded at Phoebe's freshly cleaned outfit. "So that's what stylish witches are wearing next century?"

"Hold on," Phoebe said, her concern returning, her suspicion growing. "What do you mean, 'next century'?"

Theda waved away the question. She pulled close to a dozen scrolls from her handbag and dropped them on the unmade bed next to the witches.

"As I said, I can sense things," Theda said calmly. "I'm no threat to you, Phoebe. You're looking for help, and I've come to deliver it."

Phoebe frowned. She wanted to trust Theda, but there were many magical female beings who were not witches. If only she could be sure . . .

Theda smiled. "If you're wondering exactly how I know all this about you, it was with the help of a few simple spells, like those written on the scrolls I'd like to leave with you for safekeeping."

Phoebe warily sat on the bed, Theda joining her, while keeping a reasonable distance.

"No Book of Shadows that we can get our hands on this time," Phoebe muttered, opening a couple of the scrolls and scanning the titles of the incantations written upon them in fine, flowing calligraphy. "The Binding of Names." "The Cloak of Desire." "The Forgotten Fear."

"Do you think these spells may prove useful in your current quest?" Theda asked.

"Useful, yeah," Phoebe said, barely disguising her amazement. "Looks like some pretty heavy-duty mojo!"

"You're up against some very dark forces, from what I understand. You need all the help you can get. I just wish I could stay and fight at your side, but I have a situation of my own that must be dealt with, and that battle will be fought on the desert sand, according to all the signs."

"Huh," Phoebe said. "You get looks into the future, too? Or are you part Gypsy?"

"I'm a woman of mystery, my dear. Just like you."

Phoebe wasn't sure how to respond to that one. "Mystery? Me? Sister, what you see is what you get!"

"I sense, with you, a great mystery of the heart."

"Uh-huh," Phoebe muttered. *Let's not go there, all right? Thank you.*

Theda rose unexpectedly, her gaze warily sweeping the room.

"What is it?" Phoebe asked, following the other witch's gaze, but seeing nothing at all.

"Danger," Theda said. "An old enemy has come."

Phoebe was startled by the scraping of her single window as it was suddenly raised all the way open, a familiar face peering in. It was Cole at her window, crouching outside on the fire escape. A long blade with a crimson hilt was gripped in his hand.

"*You*," Theda said icily.

Just then a groan sounded, and the wall behind the bed Phoebe thought of as her own bulged out, as if it were made of some bizarre elastic and not concrete and mortar, a pattern of pulsating gray veins reaching out from the wall.

Theda and Phoebe drew back as the wall exploded and an ivory creature that must have stood nine feet tall leaped into the room, his goatlike legs ending in hooves that tore through the mattress and collapsed the bed, his hands long blue-white talons. His eyes were black and round, his gaping maw that of an animal.

"What is that thing?" Phoebe shouted over its roars.

"One of my many enemies," Theda replied, the hint of fear in her voice revealing that she wasn't exactly prepared to deal with this threat here and now. Yet the demon facing them didn't seem to care about little things like fair play. It looked like it wanted blood.

Their blood.

"Phoebe, get down!" Cole hollered from the window.

Automatically Phoebe ducked, and the blade that had been in Cole's hand sailed across the room with blood-chilling precision—*thwunk*—to bury itself hilt-deep in the throat of the monster whose gaze was fixed on Theda!

The creature grasped at the weapon, trembling as it must have realized what was about to happen, then it exploded in a reddish black haze of otherworldly energy, leaving no shred of itself behind.

"There we go," Cole said, awkwardly climbing the rest of the way in through the open window and stumbling down in a pathetic heap. He picked himself up again, though it looked like every part of him was aching. "Score another one for the good guys." Then he set his hands on his hips. "'Course, I was hoping to use that little baby on *our* mortal enemies, but what are you going to do, right?"

Theda took a commanding step in Cole's direction. "You vanquish evil, that's what you do."

Cole's eyes widened as he took in the black-haired witch, clearly not fully recognizing her until this very moment. "*Theda!* Hi!" He gulped, the skin of his face paling. "Please don't hurt me."

"You two know each other?" Phoebe asked, shoving some of the wreckage away that had been her bed. This was just great. *How are we going to pay for the damages? And where are those scrolls?*

Whoosh!

Phoebe whirled as she heard a rush of flames and saw a pair of flaming emerald orbs gathering in Theda's open hands.

"Stand aside, Phoebe," Theda demanded. "I

have unfinished business with this wretched demon."

"Um, powerless and pathetic," Cole said. "From the future. Stuck in a body that can't cast the simplest spell."

"That's right," Phoebe said. "Cole's with us."

"And . . ." Theda's gaze moved slowly from Cole to Phoebe and back again. "The two of you were lovers."

"Cole's changed," Phoebe said truthfully, though, in her mind, that statement could be taken in any of a hundred ways.

"The mystery revealed," Theda said, turning from Cole and allowing the fiery energies in her hand to dissipate. She aimed a slender finger at the corner, where the scrolls had been thrown. "There's a spell for making things go back to the way they were before, among the incantations I brought for you."

"Really?" Cole asked, getting bolder by the second. "You mean I could get my powers back?"

"It only works on inanimate objects," Theda said. With that, she whispered, "Blessed be," and walked to the door. She opened it this time, the walruslike white-haired assistant manager standing in the hall, attempting to peer in over her luscious shoulders.

"What's with all the racket?" he asked gruffly.

Theda wiggled her fingers before his face, and a cloud of sparkling dust enveloped him. "There was no noise."

"Oh. I didn't hear anything at all."

"You need a nap."

"Going to my room right now," he agreed.

Theda looked over her shoulder, winked to Phoebe, frowned at Cole, and was gone.

"You want to tell me what that was all about?" Phoebe asked.

Cole shook his head. "No."

She knelt among the mess and scooped up the scrolls. "Tell me anyway."

"Mortal enemies. A decade of bloodsport." He scrunched his handsome features up as he made a "What of it?" motion with his hands. "Little stuff."

Yeah, with you, it's always the little stuff, isn't it? Phoebe thought. *Worm your way into our lives, make me love you, try to kill us, then confess to all of it, prove you're good . . . and go bad all over again.*

Back and forth, back and forth, until she just couldn't take it anymore.

Good or evil? Did it matter?

Little stuff.

"What?" Cole asked. "And when do I get a simple thank-you for saving your life?"

"As if anything could ever be simple with you," Phoebe said. She sifted through the spells, wondering if there was one to banish unwanted feelings. Cole had saved her life, and she was grateful. More than grateful. The entire incident had brought back memories and feelings of better times when they had fought side by side in the name of good. But good memories were painful. Right now she had some new ammunition to use against the luck demons, and she needed to focus her energies on the upcoming battle. For the first time, she was starting to think she might win.

Chapter
8

"Penny! I'm so glad you could take the time to see me today!"

Paige stood in Oscar's small office, tired after a long day of shooting. He gestured to a chair across from his desk and she sat down. She was still in her Wac costume and hadn't yet taken off her makeup. Chloe, sweetie that she was, waited outside. Paige had become accustomed to people calling her "Penny." It no longer threw her in the least. In fact, this entire acting deal was working out better than she'd expected.

Oscar's office was littered with film scripts, some stacks reaching several feet high. Photos of Oscar with noted celebrities in the entertainment industry, the business world, and even the political arena lined the walls, along with posters for his previous films. A mock-up of the one-sheet for this film sat on an easel near the window.

"Of course I'm going to make time to see you," Paige said. "You're the boss."

"I may be the one who signs the checks, but you're the one with all the power. You're the boss in this situation."

That was interesting. "Okay. Confusing, but okay."

"You see, there's something I would like to propose to you. And no, it's not marriage or anything of that sort."

Paige laughed. "You're a good guy, Oscar. I like you."

"And you're a good actress, Penny. One day, you'll be a great actress."

"Gee, thanks. Well, you know what they say about flattery, so where are you trying to get it to take ya?"

"Osiris has some terrific promotional opportunities coming up. Promotion and much more. I'm envisioning an entire slate of new productions and for that, I'm going to need major investors. I'll also need the guarantee of distribution to have our films exhibited on screens all across the world. One bit of wisdom that helped me get the backing for this studio is that connections are meaningless if you can't put on a show.

"I need the people to whom I'm appealing to feel confident that I can mount a production that's worthy of the money, the screens, of everything I'm asking them to invest. The best way I know to make them feel like they're really a part of things, to make them see exactly what they'll be getting in return for their faith in me and my vision, is to go out and give them a show. Maybe I've been inspired by my roots in vaudeville, I don't know, but I want to assemble a small troupe of actors, costumers, hair and makeup people, prop managers, set decorators, the works, who will travel with me. And when I'm in these boardrooms, I'll be able to truck the whole load of you out, with costumes, makeup, hair, and props, to play out key scenes from the upcoming films."

"Huh!" Paige said. She thought about it a moment. "It sounds to me like you could just make another movie with the kind of money you'd have to spend to do this."

"Well, that's the choice I needed to make. I could hope that this film and our next film would prove profitable enough to let our little company go on. That we could fend off not only the Ned Hawkinses of the world but also the major studios, who'd rather just buy out anyone and anything. I wanted to beat them at their own game, so I could take what might be an even greater risk, gather the troupe I've described, and either lose it all or gain more than any of us would have ever dreamed possible. At the very least, with the second option, I'd be doing what I've always done: succeeding—or failing—on my own terms."

"I can respect that," Paige said.

"The reason I said earlier that you have the power, that you would be the boss where this upcoming endeavor is concerned, is very simple: I can't pay you."

"Oh."

"For the work you're doing in this film, naturally, that's not an issue. But the best I can do, if you choose to come in with me on this deal, is fly you around the world, put you up in *fairly* decent accommodations, and offer you a role as a limited partner in Osiris Studios International."

"Wow," Paige said, sincerely impressed. "That's . . . that's a very generous offer."

But how could I possibly accept? I'm not who he thinks I am. And the real Penny Day Matthews probably wouldn't be too keen on it, either. Then there's Phoebe and Piper to consider and, well, my whole life back home.

It sure does sound like fun, though!

"Is Ned working for one of those big studios?" Paige asked. "Is that why he keeps coming around?"

"Lately he's just been coming around for you, my dear. Somehow that boy's anticipated my plans *and* the role I'd like to have you play in them."

"So he's trying to get to you through me."

"That's what I think. As far as his working for one of the studios, no, I doubt that. The last thing he wants is to be taking orders from anyone. He's trying to make a name for himself, in those circles he moves in. I'm just not going to let him make me a part of it."

Paige bit her lip, wishing she could tell Oscar at least some part of why she was seeing Ned. If only Oscar knew that she was trying to help him, and that Ned was failing miserably to get his hooks into her.

Or was he?

"Think about my offer," Oscar said. "I'd rather you not reply too quickly, one way or the other."

Paige rose, leaning over the desk and kissing Oscar on the cheek. "Oscar, what do you think the odds are of your plan actually working?"

"Don't know. Don't care. If I'd listened to even one of the people who thought they knew how good or bad my chances were of making even a single dream come true, I would have given up a long time ago. I've learned that the best way to beat the odds is to not even know you're playing them, not until the dust has settled and everything is said and done."

Piper stood outside the Hollywood Canteen. Leo had talked of this place so often, she couldn't resist the chance to come here, just once, to see what all the fuss was about.

She had taken the bus to Cahuenga Boulevard, off Sunset, and had approached the former livery stable, which had first been converted to a nightclub called The Old Barn and finally, by the efforts of John Garfield, Bette Davis, and investor Jules Stein, into this hot spot for servicemen.

And that's what it looked like: an old barn, with wide, thickly hewn wood slats making up its walls, and the words HOLLYWOOD CANTEEN FOR SERVICE MEN painted over the entrance in a charming light-hearted freehand style, like one might see at a rodeo in Piper's time. A trio of painted stars sat above the words to the left, another three to the right.

Three and three. The power of three, Piper thought.

Maybe this is a good sign. So to speak.

A teeming mass of attractive, well-dressed women were gathered outside, and it looked like those without dates were being turned away by the droves. Enlisted men had no trouble getting in, and women cooed and sighed disappointedly when no man chose to take one of them on his arm and guarantee her a way inside. Then they giggled, as if it was all a splendid game.

"The joint is jumpin' for sure tonight!" one of the women said as Piper drew closer. She could hear the rumble of music from inside, a faster beat than she would have expected.

"You know what I heard?" asked another. "I heard that Bette Davis herself had to crawl through one of the windows to get in on opening night because there wasn't any other way inside. It was that packed!"

Oh, brother, Piper thought, shaking her head and turning from the crowd. *This isn't happening. I might as well forget about it now.*

Suddenly a man slipped through the crowd, rushing up to lightly touch Piper's arm. She spun, confused. The man was in his forties, very thin, with slicked-back black hair and a hawk-like nose. He kind of looked like Basil Rathbone from the old black-and-white Sherlock Holmes films, particularly considering his wide, slightly sad dark eyes, which could narrow into an arresting gaze in a heartbeat. He wore a simple cotton suit and tie, a splash of brown to break up the beige and ivory.

Piper had changed into a basic black dress, a staple in this era *and* her own time. With it, practically any purse or handbag proved a worthwhile complement. "Can I help you?" she asked, doing her best to mask her annoyance. She wanted in, but not bad enough to play the doting little debutante like those other girls.

"Aren't you here for the auditions?" he asked.

"Pardon?"

"Auditions. For new backup singers."

"Sing?" Piper said, her throat suddenly going dry. "Me?"

"You mean you're not?" He seemed perplexed, at a loss. Then he regained himself. "I'm sorry, there's just something about you, and pardon me for saying so, I mean no offense, and I promise, I'm not being fresh . . . something that makes you different from everyone else here. A presence, if that's the right word."

She wondered if he might be sympathetic to magic, whether he knew it or not. Or if the strangeness that came as a result of her status as a witch out of time—an aura she tried to cover up—was now showing in spades. *We time-traveling witches do put out a vibe, now don't we?*

"You have a certain something that sets you apart," he said again, "the same presence as these stars who come here. So I just thought—"

"You thought right," Piper said quickly, making her mind up in that instant that masquerading as a singer was an acceptable ruse to get what she wanted, far more so than fawning over a man she didn't care about just to get something she wanted. "Auditions. Me. Yep, that's what I'm here for."

"Excellent."

He guided her through the crowd. Piper ignored the envious looks she received from those who were still being turned away and walked through the wide entrance with the man who had mistaken her for a singer.

A woman Piper thought she recognized was greeting people at the door. It wasn't until Piper had accepted a friendly handshake from the woman and walked on that Piper realized she'd just met Lana Turner!

Leo wasn't kidding, there really were movie stars here.

"I'm afraid I must take my leave of you, my dear," the hawk-nosed man said, smiling with comforting warmth as he led her to a crush of people with their backs to the hallway. "I'll call on you when it's time!"

He slipped between a pair of chatting couples and disappeared from view. Piper made her way in, amazed at how crowded the place actually was. She had no idea how people could find one another here.

That thought made her pause.

Is that why I came? she wondered uneasily. Was she here not just to experience firsthand a place that had meant so much to Leo, but to actually *find* him? To set her gaze upon the living, breathing man that he been before he had shipped out, before he had been . . .

Before he became a Whitelighter?

The press of the crowd drove those thoughts away. She hugged the edge of the great dance floor, sidling past groups of servicemen laughing and joking in the bleachers. From what a few of them said, she learned it was Xavier Cugat who led the band in a rousing rumba, making the entire place explode with laughter, song, and dance!

She had seen old films of couples swing dancing, but she had never realized how beautiful and exciting it was to watch up close, and how, well . . . sexy.

The walls were covered with murals. Piper

found some of the styles familiar, but she couldn't put names to any of them. Some were realistic, Norman Rockwell–like renditions of the boys at war; others were cartoons. Easing though the crowd, she passed a pretty blonde whom a handful of army boys were making a fuss over.

"Okay, blondie," Piper muttered, anxious to turn her thoughts in any other direction. "What makes you so special?"

"That's Miss Dinah Shore," a friendly, freckle-faced, red-haired boy with glasses told her in a deep southern drawl. He sidled up to her with a winning smile and an army uniform that was not yet decorated.

It was funny: Outside she had made the decision not to hang on some man's arm, and she didn't know this boy at all ("boy" was a wrong term to use—he was eighteen at least, a man about to go and fight for his country), but she felt at ease in his presence. She also had a sense that he wasn't normally so easygoing around the ladies.

What the heck, as long as he was around, she wouldn't get hit on by anyone else. And there *was* something about him.

Something familiar . . .

"A bunch of us were in the other night from the army hospital, and she was just as sweet as could be," the young man, whom she thought of as "Red," told her with a broad smile, instants before he downed a good half of the doughnut he clutched.

"Is that right?" Piper was instantly alert. Leo had been a medic.

"Yes, ma'am." He winked and told her his name—which she, much to her embarrassment, immediately forgot—and his division.

Leo's division.

Was that why this boy seemed familiar? Had Leo spoken of him?

Leo's here, Piper thought, her heart suddenly thundering. *He might be, anyway.*

"Eddie Cantor's taking the stage later on," Red informed her, putting one hand on his chest while reaching out with the other. He stretched it out as far as he could without whacking some dancing soldier, or his lovely partner, in the head. Attempting a swagger, he lightly crooned, "The coffee could be sweeter, but I'm not in the dumps, 'cause every time she hugs me, it's like two extra lumps!"

Red's eyes opened wide with that one, his face and ears suddenly flushing bright enough to match his hair as he totally embarrassed himself. "Oops! Sorry."

Piper smiled. Red was a gentleman in the making, if a little rough around the edges. "That's okay."

"It could have been worse. I could have done some of that raunchy Red Skelton and totally humiliated myself. As it is, I'm just ninety percent of the way there."

The music swelled.

"Let's check this place out," Piper said, speaking loudly to be heard over the now pounding beat of the band. She had to admit, she was impressed. Some of these songs really rocked.

She wasn't sure if Red heard her, but he followed as she turned and wove her way between the press of laughing, dancing couples. They were so sexy, yet so innocent; an impossible mix, but there it was. She spied impossibly good-looking men in waiters' outfits serving drinks. They were movie stars, too!

A sign behind a nearby counter where stacks of doughnuts and drinks waited on trays read: FOOD AND REFRESHMENTS FREE!

She could have *sworn* that Humphrey Bogart was among the kitchen help.

Some of the boys were dancing with actresses whose faces were so familiar . . . was that Bette Davis herself?

This place was incredible!

The music segued into a tune with a less urgent beat, allowing the couples surrounding her to slow dance, though most kept their bodies a chaste distance from each other. Piper imagined holding the Leo of this time and dancing with him to this music, wondering if he would look at her and feel even a shred of the love he would one day come to have for her.

This is crazy. It's wrong. I've got to get out of here before I do something I'm going to regret.

Red caught her looking around. "We're just

farm boys, you know. Not all of us. Some from small towns, others from the lower side of big cities. The thing is, here we're all the same. Even us and these celebrities. It's like the stars come down from the heavens."

"Maybe it's where angels come from," Piper murmured, thinking of the man who would one day be her Whitelighter—and her husband.

"If you're including yourself in that, miss, I'd say you're correct."

Miss? Oh! Piper realized she hadn't volunteered her name when he had given his.

Of course, maybe that was for the best. If Leo was here, if she saw him, or worse, told him what was going to happen . . .

Then a familiar head of close-cropped blond hair came into view a dozen feet off, near the bleachers, and Piper tensed.

Was that him? Was that Leo across the room? Was it?

Suddenly a man's hand was on her shoulder. She spun, lifting her hands as if to use her power, her heart racing, and she saw the kind gentleman who had let her inside the club. Red stepped back, amused.

"You're up," he said, gesturing at the stage. She saw a shiny microphone stand glinting in the lights and allowed herself to be ushered over to it, Red leading a round of applause as she skittered up a small flight of wooden steps and was placed directly before the oddly shaped microphone. It looked like the handset of a walkie-talkie.

The hawk-faced man withdrew, and the band-leader, a rounded, Hispanic man with a dark mustache and an encouraging smile, whispered the name of a tune that must have been on every-one's lips in this era. The music started, another slow tune, and the bandleader nodded . . . then nodded again . . . and again.

It was time for her to sing, and she felt ridicu-lously self-conscious, just as she had when Leo had tried to make her take the stage at P3. And if that *was* Leo, and he got a good look at her now, might that somehow upset the natural flow of events through time later? Or was she using that as an excuse to dodge being humiliated in front of a roomful of strangers?

"I'm sorry," Piper said. She ran from the stage, barreling past a crowd of confused and disappointed faces, doing her best to hide her own as she passed Red and the boys with him, one of whom might have been Leo, and fled the canteen.

Paige paced across the narrow strip of floor that was available to her in the hotel room she shared with her three sisters. Piper and Phoebe sat together on one bed, Cole on the other.

"I got an idea of what Ned was talking about that day when he said Oscar was going interna-tional," Paige said. She went on to tell the others of Oscar's plans. "I just can't see why Ned wants in on the deal. What's his end of things? What does he get out of it?"

"It could be quite a bit," Cole said softly, thinking this through. "I heard some talk today of someone setting up a network to traffic in exactly the kind of magical artifacts Hawkins and his friends seem to have gotten their hands on."

"Trafficking?" Phoebe asked.

"There's a black market for everything, and a lot of pretty nasty types scattered all over the world right now. Hitler's *known* to have been obsessed with this stuff." He shook his head. "*Is* obsessed. Sorry. I keep forgetting what year it is."

"Okay, but why would they need Osiris?" Paige asked.

"To transport the artifacts," Cole said. "They could be made to look like movie props easily enough, slip right by customs."

"That doesn't track," Piper said. She had seemed distracted until now, but talk of the war had brought her fully into the conversation. "Demons can shimmer to and from any place they want."

"Sure," Cole said. "But would a demon want to, with that kind of firepower? It's not safe. You have to be really careful, take all sorts of special precautions, if you're planning on using magic anywhere near the artifacts. But box 'em up, put 'em in a crate or someone's luggage, and it's no big deal."

"That's just weird," Paige complained.

"Hey, I don't make the rules."

"Let's say you're right," Phoebe said. "What can we do to change Hawkins's plans?"

Cole smiled. "Funny you should ask. I just *happen* to have one or two ideas. . . ."

Chapter

9

Cole was jolted awake by the blare of an alarm clock. He shuddered, and attempted to will the ringing clock out of existence.

Nothing happened.

Growling with frustration, Cole turned over, anchoring himself on one elbow, and mashed his fist onto the small alarm. The off button sat atop its round little ceramic head.

"Ow!" he hollered, a surprising pain reaching up from the side of his hand as he hit the clock at an angle, knocking it aside, and bruising himself in the process.

Cole sat up in bed, nursing his aching hand, the golden glow of early morning blazing in through the thin curtains covering the small window in his room. Hunger immediately seized him, an insistent, immense, and strangely powerful hand working its way through his stomach, gripping and squeezing him hard, or so it felt. His throat was dry; his breath, as he could smell it on his pillow, very bad indeed.

First things first. He sat up, smiling, and said to no one in particular, "Okay. I want Belgian waffles, and an omelet with ham, bacon, and onions, the bacon lightly crisped, orange juice freshly squeezed, and strong coffee."

He snapped his fingers, expecting a tray with everything he had ordered to magically appear in his lap.

No such luck.

He snapped again. And yet again.

"Oh," he groused, rubbing his hand over his face and feeling stubble. "That's right."

Cole growled, low and deep in his throat, and set to the hard work of making himself presentable.

This was a big day, after all. The meeting was set with the Hawkins boys for just after sundown, and that gave him the better part of the day to take care of last-minute details, like spreading rumors about the Wyatt gang to whoever would listen, and doing it the right way, of course. There was no sense in just going to thug hangouts and saying he'd heard this or that about how bad and mean the Wyatts were. No, the best thing to do was to go in, act relieved, like he had just been let off the hook for some nasty business that had been weighing on him for weeks, then start talking about what the Wyatt gang wasn't, and what they didn't have.

That sounded crazy, of course, but it was all in how you did it. The key was in being highly specific. You didn't say, "I heard those guys have connections to all kinds of heavy hitters in the demon realm, but, nah, it's all bull."

Instead, saying, "Those Wyatts really had us running scared. We heard they had a hundred fourteen higher demons for lieutenants, and connections with forty-one demon dimensions." Then he'd see whoever he was shooting the breeze with simply tense up. It was inevitable. The person he was talking with would start repeating those numbers after a while. "A hundred fourteen high demons for lieutenants?" would be the frightened query. And Cole could come back with, "Well, that's what I heard, but it's not true."

"A hundred fourteen, though. That's a lot."

"It'd be a lot if there was anything to it, but I'm telling you, no hundred fourteen higher demon lieutenants, no connections with forty-one demon dimensions. Just a load of bull."

And he'd leave that victim of misinformation quaking and move on to the next at another hangout, on and on, throughout the day.

He bathed in the slippery tub, his body still aching from the beating he'd taken when he'd approached some underworld types the wrong way. As the Source, just wandering into a demon dive and throwing your weight around to get information was one thing. Even as Cole Turner back from the demon realms with more power than he knew what to do with, or as an attorney, possibly the most frightening of all, pure bluster and bravado might have been enough to pull it off. But he felt powerless, his humanity and mortality radiating from him no matter how hard he tried to hide it.

What he needed for this meeting tonight was power. Raw, merciless power.

Fortunately he knew just where to find it.

Sighing, he dried himself off, going back to the ho-hums of human existence in 1942, and actually finding the exotic nature of the whole thing kind of exciting.

He opened the armoire and picked out his clothes for the day. Cole chose a Finchley 5th Avenue number, a light-gray-striped wool flannel double-breasted suit complemented by a clean and newly pressed white cotton shirt. The Wembley tie he took down was gray and beige with an art deco swing design. He snatched up gray shoes and topped off the ensemble with a natty gray fedora. Thank god Phoebe had deigned—however reluctantly—to shop with him.

He laid the clothes on the bed, then went about the many mundane tasks that were set before him, yelping again as he cut himself shaving.

Though he couldn't believe he was even thinking this, he wished Leo, with his White-lighter healing powers, were there. He had been the Source, for heaven's sake. This was as humili-ating as it was embarrassing.

Or maybe it was just humbling—exactly the kind of humbling he should go through if he were ever to win Phoebe back. He said that he still loved her, that his love drove his actions. Now it was time to put up or shut up.

Still, he just couldn't believe how much work went into just being human!

It was too bad Phoebe hadn't accepted his offer to bunk with him. She'd have enjoyed see-ing him cut down to size like this.

He sighed. There were *lots* of reasons he wished she were with him now, more than she would ever believe. First and foremost, he still loved her more than anything else in the world.

Yet she had wounded his pride in so many ways, on so many occasions. He wanted her, yes, and he had done terrible things. But Phoebe liked to forget little details about stuff: For example, the only reason he took the evil that was the Source into him was to save her and her sisters. And the whole time it was a part of him, he had wanted that evil driven out.

There really was only so much of her hostility and judgment that he could take.

"Well, you know what they say," he whispered

to himself. "If you can't have what you want, and you can't have what you need, the least you can do is have a little fun."

Once he was dressed, Cole went to the window and looked out on the street below.

"Showtime," he whispered, looking out on the unsuspecting city and smiling as if he were about to consume everyone and everything in his line of vision.

And perhaps, in a way, he would.

The sky was crimson as Paige turned on the bath in Ned's spacious master bathroom. Her long legs eased from the silk robe she had borrowed, and her hair was piled up and safely secured in an ivory towel. Two of Ned's servants were with her, one helping her get the temperature just so, the other tooling through radio stations for her, pausing at each and waiting for her to give a yea or nay. She had been to Ned's mansion in the Malibu hills three times now, never once staying overnight, of course. But she had mentioned her love of long baths, and he told her to take advantage of the facilities whenever she wished. He was out on business, and Paige told his butler that she wished to spend a few hours "sumptuously soaking" while awaiting his return.

The bathtub itself was marble and jade; the bathroom and the entire mansion, like something from an MGM movie she might spot on one of the nostalgia channels. Great stone lions greeted visitors as they walked up the steps to the main doors. There was a ballroom, a dining hall, an enormous pool, a game room that had a tiny office just off it, and a study that was always locked and that Ned never allowed Paige to enter. She tried orbing in a couple of times, but it was mystically sealed.

Poking a single perfect toe in the hot, bubbling waters, Paige said, "The water's fine!"

Withdrawing her toe and standing elegantly next to the bath, Paige told the second servant that the jazz station he had just selected would be more than adequate for her needs. When both were gone, she locked the door, slid off her robe, and removed the towel from her hair. She eased herself into the bath, which felt heavenly, and held her breath as she dunked herself, wetting her hair.

Then she got out, put on her robe, and orbed away in a shimmer of blue-white light.

She reappeared in her room in the Towers, a very different kind of wardrobe laid out for her. Phoebe and Piper had already changed, with Chloe fussing about them, handling a few last-minute details. The young woman didn't even jump around an orb anymore, which was nice. She had the makings of a truly terrific Wiccan.

"My alibi's in place," Paige said, tossing off her robe and trying not to think about what she might do if their imminent encounter did not go as planned.

In moments she was dressing for war.

Banzaf, the demon who was called Barrish in his human guise, sat uneasily beside Ned Hawkins in the younger man's new Caddy. Banzaf had the same gray-blue eyes as Hawkins, but there the resemblance ceased. Banzaf's face was olive colored and riddled with pockmarks. His features were blocky, intimidating—but with a single smile he could look like a kind and doting uncle.

Ned loved him like a father, there was no denying it. And he valued Banzaf's opinion, though he didn't always follow the older man's advice.

"This may be more than we can handle," the advisor said, referring to the meeting he had set up in response to the demon Belthazor's summons. He was unnerved. What was Belthazor up to? And would the demon assassin betray Ned and the others?

"I've asked around about the Wyatt gang. Word on the street—"

"Still just words," Ned said sharply. "I believe what I can see."

"I've seen Belthazor in action. It wasn't pretty. He's as powerful as they come."

"Strong enough to resist our powers?"

"Quite possibly."

Ned smiled. "Then it's good we're not relying just on them, isn't it?"

Banzaf nodded. Still, he couldn't shake the sense of unease he felt as he followed Ned out of the car, and joined with the other members of their demonic gang, which had gathered for this little meeting.

If anything, as he eyed the alley where Cole Turner promised to be at this hour, his discomfort and unease were growing into something very much like fear.

In the dead center of the alley, four identically dressed figures waited. They wore black suits with white pinstripes, thin black ties, and black hats with white hatbands. Cole was one of them. The other three were the Charmed Ones, each disguised to look like a "tough guy."

Emphasis on the "guy" part.

The witches' bosoms had been flattened down with tightly pinned strips of cloth, and each wore fake facial hair, small moles, and other bits of makeup to disguise their features. Paige had been covered up the most, a goatee and a short black wig obscuring her looks on the off chance Ned was able to get within a dozen feet of her, which she was hoping he would not.

"Cole, are you sure about this?" Phoebe asked. "We can still back out."

He almost laughed. "Come on, Phoebes,

what's the worst that can happen? Hawkins figures out I'm human, grabs me, takes me somewhere you guys can't locate, and tortures me for days before killing me horribly? I thought that would pretty much make your day."

"Don't say that. I don't want you hurt, Cole. I just want you gone. I want to live my life without you being a part of it. There's a difference."

"Not for me. A life without you isn't one that's worth living." He nodded to the end of the alley, where nattily dressed figures were gathering, then turned to look in the other direction. More figures were peeling themselves away from the walls. "Besides, it's too late. Company's arrived."

"Paige could still orb us out."

Cole shook his head. "Not a chance. I've been looking forward to this all day."

Ned Hawkins approached, his soldiers trailing behind him. He stopped three paces before Cole and looked him up and down with a contemptuous grin. Then he gazed at Cole's three lieutenants.

"Four of you. That's it?" Ned Hawkins asked incredulously. The older guy who was his advisor remained a half dozen steps behind him, eyeing the quartet warily.

"That's all it takes," Cole said.

"I brought a few more soldiers, myself. It makes me feel luck's on my side, know what I mean?"

"Whatever," Cole said, angling his head back

a little in the direction of the disguised Charmed Ones. "The way I figure things, if you've got enough firepower, luck doesn't really come into it."

An array of metal clacking sounded. Cole averted his gaze long enough to see that the demons now had guns in their hands.

Hawkins yawned. "Looks like we've got you beat on that front too."

"*Please.*" Cole shot him a look that said, *You've got to be kidding.*

Hawkins appeared amused. "No guns?"

Cole gestured and his "muscle" drew a little closer. "Don't believe in guns. Don't need 'em, either."

"Fine," Ned said, glancing up at the windows and rooftops bracing him. There could, of course, be dozens of demons up above under Cole's control, lying in wait to ambush them. But he still wasn't worried. "You called this meeting. Out of respect to Belthazor, I came. Now what did you want to talk about?"

"I want in on your action. Simple as that," Cole said.

"What action are we talking about?" Ned asked, his confident expression unchanging.

"Let's see . . . the sword of Damocles, the actual one, not the figurative . . . the Rosetta stone . . . the spear of Destiny, just to name a few."

Ned flinched. "You're bluffing."

"Please. You got your hands on the most powerful mystical objects in the history of the world—*this* world, anyway—stumbling on them by pure, dumb luck, would be my guess. And all you can think to do with them is to sell them to the highest bidder. You're lucky I was the one who found out about this. There are a lot of demons out there who would have just come for your head and taken what they wanted instead of working out a deal. The thing is, I'm a lot like you. Smarter and better looking, sure, but I don't like being held down by the demon hierarchy either."

"You want power," Ned whispered.

"Don't you? I think we'd make terrific partners. I've got the vision and the muscle; you've got the knack for making things happen. But first things first. I want to see the artifacts."

Their gazes were locked. Hawkins was silent, thinking it over. Cole watched him, knowing it all came down to this moment. He had considered having the Charmed Ones put on a display of sheer force to help make his argument a little more convincing, but, in any major deal he had ever worked, it all came down to who blinked first. Getting pushy like that might have made Cole appear desperate, or afraid. The only way he could make this bluff convincing was with sheer strength of will and the basis of his solid reputation. He had to tap into the depths of inner darkness he had told Phoebe were long gone from his soul; he had to make Hawkins fear that he would crush him like a bug if it came to it. It was amusing to him to have things play out this way.

But if he loved Phoebe, and wanted to prove to her that he wasn't evil anymore, should this amuse him so much? Were all of his assertions really his? Even to himself?

That instant of doubt cost Cole. Hawkins grinned and stepped back, breaking eye contact.

"You know what?" Ned asked victoriously, a streak of cruelty in his voice. "I want to see who I'm really dealing with here. Show me Belthazor."

Cole laughed, his casual manner proving to be far more unnerving than any black-hearted posturing. But inwardly, he knew the game was lost. He took one last stab at the charade. "These days I only take that form when I'm getting ready to kill. I'm not about to get my hands dirty with losers like you."

The two men stared at each other, then Ned turned away.

"To hell with this," Ned said without a trace of humor or irony in his voice. "Forget the guns, that'd be too easy. But kill 'em all!"

"To orb or not to orb?" Paige asked as the supernatural gangsters came running. "That *is* the question—"

"I say we end this here," Phoebe said. "We have innocents to protect, and the best way to do that is to vanquish these suckers here and now."

"Fine by me," Cole said, drawing a pair of shining three-pronged sais from under his coat. He whipped them to each side and they suddenly came alive with crackling white fire. "I may be human, but that doesn't mean I can't use these."

"Fine," Piper said, raising both hands. "Time to kick some demon butt."

Piper turned so that each of her hands faced a different set of oncoming demons. She let loose her magic, but instead of blowing up any of the demons she had aimed at, she exploded two trash cans, a stack of old crates, and the front windshield of an abandoned car that sat on concrete blocks a few yards from the demons.

What on earth? Why wasn't her magic working properly?

"This is going to be harder than I thought," said Piper angrily. She summoned all the power she could and sent out two more blasts—with similar results. This time chunks of brick came raining down from somewhere close, and the witches had to duck and dodge to avoid being struck in the head by the debris.

"This was your brilliant idea! Do something!" Piper yelled at Phoebe.

"Maybe whatever spell they're using only works to protect against magic. Let's see." Phoebe walked over to a nearby garbage can, grabbed its lid and hurled it at the first group of demons led by Ned.

A sudden, powerful gust of wind rose out of nowhere, striking the lid in midflight, averting its route. One of the demons reached out and caught the lid in his huge hands, grinning as he crushed it to the size of a tin can. Then the wind vanished as quickly as it had appeared.

What were the odds of that happening?

"Well, great," Paige said, despairingly. "We can't even throw things at them."

Cole whipped his sais through the air. Then he loosed lightning bolts at the demons—and had to duck as the crackling magical energies ricocheted against the walls above or to either side of his intended victims, and boomeranged back at him and the Charmed Ones!

He said, "This is going to be the shortest turf war in history unless we can drop that protection spell they're using. Can any of you see an object that might be powering their spell? Anything?"

Now the demons were strolling along, enjoying the looks of fear they were creating by drawing this out.

The Charmed Ones scanned the demons for any kind of magical object. Phoebe finally caught sight of something. One of the demons, who was wearing a brown coat, held an amulet that had a huge green glowing crystal in its center.

"The demon in brown, he has an amulet," shouted Phoebe.

Paige glared at the demon, concentrated, and said, "Amulet." The amulet immediately orbed into Paige's right hand. Whatever was affecting Paige's magic didn't seem to extend to orbing.

"Hah, now *we* have the protection," said Paige, keeping her voice low and gruff in case Ned heard her. "I wonder how you use this," she muttered.

Before anyone could answer her, the ladder from the fire escape over her head suddenly came loose, slicing down like a guillotine's blade. Phoebe leaped at Paige, knocking her sister out of the way as the loose ladder slammed to the ground, falling on the witches. The amulet was thrown from Paige's hand and it smashed against the nearby wall.

"At least neither of us has magical protection now," said Phoebe, helping Paige to her feet.

Ned was laughing his head off. "Got some real muscle there," Ned said. "Nice. All it takes is a little bit of bad luck, though. Then it's the old, 'bigger they are, harder they fall.'"

"Helps if you don't have far to go," Cole muttered.

Ned smiled and invoked another spell. This time the bars on the windows of the buildings came to life, pulled themselves free and soared toward Cole. They looked like mystically charged javelins. Cole raised his sais and deflected each one as it came toward him.

Then the howling mass of attackers was on them, fighting hand to hand. Phoebe levitated and kicked, getting in a lucky shot that sent one demon falling back onto Cole's outstretched sais. With a holler, he exploded in a cloud of flame.

"One down," Phoebe said.

"Yeah, only four or five thousand to go!" Piper yelled.

"We need to orb out of here," Cole said. "They're using their luck powers against us!"

"Yeah, like they're giving us much of a chance," Paige growled.

Phoebe nodded. She had memorized several of the spells Theda had given them, and, with the information Paige had acquired, knew that one in particular would come in handy in a fight like this.

"Just buy me a couple of seconds," Phoebe said, easing away from the fight.

"We'll do our best," Piper said as she blew up an abandoned car a demon had sent flying toward her. Then they were all ducking fenders, doors, and engine parts that whirred by like shrapnel.

Phoebe recited the Binding of Names, inserting the name "Banzaf" into her incantation. The instant she finished, Ned's advisor stiffened, his eyes going milk white. Suddenly she could feel their connection. He was like a puppet, and she could pull his strings. Fortunately for her, the demon's inherent luck powers hadn't made this spell go awry. It was weird, though— everything Piper, Paige, and Cole tried was undone by the natural protection of good fortune the demons enjoyed, but Phoebe had twice been able to attack successfully. She wasn't complaining, but she also couldn't help noticing the disparity and wondering what had caused it.

"Banzaf," Phoebe commanded, "do me a favor and kick some demon backside, will ya?"

Banzaf turned on his own men, roaring as he went into a rage and began tearing his frightened and confused allies into little bits.

Cole, in the meantime, was fighting off Ned and his demons with his sais and his martial arts training, but Phoebe could see that he was tiring. He wouldn't be able to hold out much longer on his own against all these demons with only a couple of mystical weapons.

"We need to hurry," said Phoebe.

The Charmed Ones joined hands and Paige was ready to orb—but she couldn't reach Cole, and they weren't about to leave him behind.

"Banzaf, get these guys off our backs!" Phoebe shouted. "Now!"

Without hesitation, Banzaf spun and tore into the demons who had Cole pinned down. Finally free, Cole brought his sais around and blasted in the general direction of his enemies. Banzaf hollered as twin streaks of lightning pierced his chest, and he exploded in a shower of fiery energies that threw everyone back. Every remaining demon, including Ned, fell away from the fight, staring at Cole in shock.

Cole stumbled into Paige's reach, but she hesitated before orbing them to safety. The look in Ned's eyes as she stared down at the scorched pavement where his mentor had stood was horrible. Ned knelt on the spot, his calm demeanor cracking, his anger mixing with grief as he then stood up, straightened his coat, and wiped dirt from his pant leg. He pointed at Cole.

"You won't believe the way I'm gonna make you suffer for that."

Paige orbed them back to their hotel room. It took each of them a moment to adjust to being out of the thick of battle.

"I have to move to get back to the mansion so I'm there when Ned gets back," said Paige as she quickly took off the men's clothes she had been wearing, removed and washed off the rest of the makeup, and put her silk robe back on. Then, without even looking at her sisters, she orbed back to the Hawkins mansion, removed the robe, and jumped into the now freezing-cold water of the bath.

The bracing water was exactly what she needed. *We didn't do anything wrong*, she told herself. *Ned's evil. He's got to be stopped.*

Even so, she felt a shudder pass through her that had nothing to do with frigid waters.

She knew that Ned would be in pain, terrible pain, over this.

And that knowledge also made her hurt somewhere deep inside.

Chapter

10

"What are you doing here?"

Paige stood, arms at her sides, eyes wide with surprise, standing beside the billiard table in his lavish game room. Her hair was still wet from the tub. "We had a date, remember? I came earlier to take a nice soak in your tub while I was waiting. Got here a couple of hours ago."

He stared at her, his expression wondrous, despairing, hopeful, and mournful, a kaleidoscope of contradictions. He looked like he had just lost his best friend.

"Are you okay?" she asked.

His expression softened. "You're not going to be seeing Barrish anymore."

"What happened?"

Ned hesitated. He *almost* told her. Paige was certain that he was right on the brink of telling her everything, including his true demonic nature and whatever had happened tonight.

He said quietly, "Something bad happened."

"Oh, honey, I'm so sorry," she said, her hands settling comfortably with a familiar ease and grace on his chest. "Do you want to talk about it?"

"No," he said, his right hand touching both of hers, drawing them together and giving them a gentle squeeze. Despite his strength, he displayed a surprising tenderness.

She was amazed at how she responded to him! She *wanted* to ease his pain. Looking into his eyes, she saw it again: a desire to reveal himself fully to her, to fix it so that there would be no further secrets between them.

That should have thrilled her. It meant she was getting close to him, close enough to learn not only how to vanquish the entire clan of luck demons, but also where they kept their cache of powerful mystical items, one or more of which could have the energy necessary to get the Charmed Ones back to their own time.

Still, she felt bad for him. If they had just met, if she didn't *know* what she did of him, she might think he was a good man. Misguided maybe, set on a path he was told he had no other choice but to follow, doing things he thought were right because no one had ever shown him another way. At his essence, a good man. Or someone with the potential to be a good man.

Come on, Paige. Not a man. *Demon. Bad guy.*

Paige had to repress a shudder. "Is there anything I can do?"

Ned looked away from her. "I think I just . . . I need to get some, uh, business affairs in order. Do some work. That'll make me feel better."

"I understand," Paige said, relieved, yet so very torn. She wanted to comfort him—she wanted to see his evil stopped, his line vanquished.

He kissed her, and his lips were cold, *so* icy cold they might have burned. Her heart went nova, an exploding sun.

"Good night, Penny," he said softly, turning from her, leaving her shaking slightly. He crossed to his study, unlocked the door, went inside the darkened room, and shut the door behind himself.

He did *not* lock the door, Paige carefully observed, forcing her emotions under control. *This is all part of going undercover. You've seen it in a thousand TV shows and movies. The flame burns brightly, and you're drawn to it.*

Is this what it was like for Phoebe, with Cole?

Paige waited for one of his servants to arrive, her coat in hand, but the elderly man appeared without her coat and he seemed agitated.

"Is Master Hawkins in his study?" the servant asked.

Paige nodded. The servant rapped on the door, calling out to Ned that he had an urgent call from overseas. The study door opened, Ned glancing to Paige in surprise.

"I'll find my own way out, no problem," she said.

His smile was thin as he pulled the door shut but did *not* lock it. Paige had to hide her excitement over this surprising move.

"I have your coat in the foyer," the servant said to Paige. "I'll see you out."

Paige accompanied both men to the foyer, Ned briskly leaving her behind with nothing more than the lightest touch of his fingers against hers—*electric, exciting*—and then he was gone.

Outside, one of Ned's drivers had pulled up in a black Cadillac, the moonlight glinting off its hood. The solidly built man came around to open the passenger door and Paige approached him warmly.

"Petey, would you be a sweetie and bring around one of Ned's roadsters? Maybe the twenty-nine Ford? He said I could borrow one of them if I wanted, and I so feel like driving myself tonight."

"Of course," the driver said.

In minutes she was motoring away, and once she was a few safe miles distant, confident that she had not been followed, Paige pulled the roadster off the road, onto a winding shoulder thick with tree cover, and got out.

The door to Ned's study had been locked in more ways than one. Mystical seals prevented her from orbing inside. What if those seals were connected to the actual lock on the door, which Ned had, for the first time, left *unlocked*?

There was only one way to find out.

Okay, Paige, she thought, steadying herself. *Here goes nothin'!*

She orbed inside. Within ten minutes she had gone through his private files and found the answers to practically all their questions about Hawkins, his people, and the artifacts he was trafficking in.

Cole had been right. Ned was in the middle of something bigger than he could possibly handle.

The only question left in her mind is what would happen to him after they had taken the artifacts and ruined his plans. Oscar and Osiris would be saved, but Ned and his clan would be ruined.

That is, if she and her sisters weren't forced to vanquish them first.

Hearing movement outside the study, Paige orbed away.

It wouldn't be until the middle of the night that she would wake and wonder if she had remembered to turn off the small desk light by his confidential files, which she had turned on to be able to read Ned's papers. She told herself that she was being paranoid; of course she had turned it off.

But she was wrong.

Piper couldn't believe she once again stood across the street from the Hollywood Canteen. This time, instead of trying to get in through the front door, which was, yet again, clogged with happy GIs and tons of attractive women, she went around to the back. She had several parcels in her arms from Schwab's, and she hoped against hope that they would prove to be her ticket in.

She wore an unassuming outfit, her "secret weapon" for the evening packed in the bottom box.

A couple of burly security guys waited at the back door.

"Delivery from Schwab's," Piper said, struggling to hold her voice steady. *This is crazy. I shouldn't be doing this!*

"Give it here," the closer of the two men ordered, holding out his meaty hands.

"Sorry, fella. I'm from the kitchen. I'm part of the full meal deal."

The two guys exchanged confused looks.

"I've got all the fixings for a special dessert for the boys, but my boss doesn't want the secret recipe getting out," Piper fibbed. "So I need to get in, get myself a little counter space, and get cooking with this stuff so it'll be ready in time."

They appeared to be buckling, but weren't quite convinced.

"Fine," Piper said with a shrug. "No skin off my nose. What are your names?"

Without hesitation, the two men gave them.

"Great!" Piper said. "Now I can tell my boss who it was that kept Mr. Garfield from having his favorite dessert in his own club."

Both men drew in sharp breaths at this. They exchanged looks again, worried glances this time, and without another word, parted and opened the door for her.

"Thanks, fellas," she said. "You guys are a couple of good eggs. I'll be sure to let the boss know."

When she looked back, the men were beaming.

"Didja hear that?" one asked the other.

"You bet," his partner replied. "Maybe we'll get to meet Lana Turner or one o' them famous dames!"

Piper heard the door close behind her as she entered the vast kitchen. It was a beehive of activity, just as she had guessed it would be. Not one person took notice of her as she slid the boxes she carried onto a supply shelf against the back wall and yanked the bottom one free.

Finding a restroom was simple enough. She changed into the slinky black dress she'd brought, then slipped through the kitchen doors, narrowly avoiding a frantic server, and sashayed onto the main dance floor. Suddenly a man in a tan uniform slipped in front of her. He was skinny, pimply faced, and nervous as all get out.

"What are you doing here tonight?" the soldier asked, smiling too broadly as he tried to run his hand through his hair and encountered a scalp shaved so close, leaving only a sheen of fuzz, that he needn't have bothered.

"Something really stupid," Piper said with a sigh. "I'm looking for someone."

The soldier straightened up. "Private Michael J. O'Malley, at your service, ma'am! Care for a dance?"

"No, I mean . . . a friend."

"Oh!" Private O'Malley said. "What's her name? What does she look like? Maybe I could help."

"It's not a her."

His shoulders sagged, the wind knocked out of him. "Oh."

Piper had rationalized coming here tonight because she wasn't using any powers or spells to bring about her desired outcome. Yet she was also very aware of the danger that was posed by messing around with the timeline. Leo was meant to go overseas. Meant to fall while doing his duty as a medic. It was that act, along with so many other unselfish things he had done in his life, that earned him his wings as a Whitelighter. If she warned him about what was coming, if she found some way of convincing him to do even one thing differently so he wouldn't die in battle, what would it mean to all their lives? And to the lives of all those he had helped through the decades as a Whitelighter?

"Miss?" Private O'Malley asked with great concern.

"Sorry," Piper said, suddenly feeling unsteady on her feet. The young private took her arm and guided her to a nearby table, where he handed her a glass of ice water.

Thanking him, she took it gladly. The enormity of what she'd been contemplating had threatened to overwhelm her. Still, if she could just see him once, see him as he had been, if she could touch him, dance one dance with him . . .

It was wrong. She knew it was wrong.

"I hope I haven't done anything to upset you," the private said.

"No, you haven't," Piper said, taking in the band, all the happy couples on the dance floor, the mass of servicemen in the bleachers.

Leo might, or might not, be among them. When she had been here last time, she had met a man from his unit who had talked as if Leo had come to this place. When she had thought about it, the whole thing made sense to her. They were in this time and this place because it was somewhere Leo had associated with safety, and, according to the soldier she spoke with, his unit was due to ship out tomorrow. Why wouldn't he join his pals for one last night here at the Canteen?

The band finished its latest song. Piper hadn't been paying much attention to it, but she did manage to overhear the bandleader chatting with another musician. They were going to take a break. Good. That just might make it easier for her to circulate and catch a glimpse of—

Piper gripped the edge of her table and set down her water glass. There he was!

Leo walked toward the exit with a handful of his fellow soldiers, laughing, patting one another on the back . . . yet there was a touch of sadness in Leo's eyes. Piper was clear across the club, she couldn't really see him well enough to know if she was reading his expression right or not. It was closer to something she *felt* as she looked at him.

He was not the Leo she knew. Not quite. His courage and strength was there, but his unflagging hope for the future was not as strong as she had always known it to be. Something was missing from him.

Suddenly it all made sense to Piper. She knew exactly why she had been drawn here, why she *had* to see Leo before he left.

There was a chance that she and her sisters would fail, and they would never return to their own time. If that happened, this would be her one and only chance to ever see him again.

"That song," Piper said softly. "It wasn't recorded until 1944, but he remembered it from before he shipped out."

"Pardon?" the private beside her asked.

This time there was no hesitation. She bolted from her chair, crossed to the open mike, and sang the first few bars of the song Leo had drawn so much comfort from, so much hope.

"Gonna take a sentimental journey," she sang. "Gonna set my heart at ease. . . ."

As she sang, all heads turned, and a spotlight was shone on her. She wasn't afraid in the slightest. Leo had given them all the strength to do so many things that none of them thought they ever could, and it was all because he believed in them so strongly, because his hope and his faith were unshakable. This was why she needed to be here. This was the gift she needed to give back to him, bringing their own journey of love full circle.

"Seven . . . that's the time we leave, at seven," she sang, Leo now little more than a fuzzy figure in the far distance through the brilliant light that had been cast upon her. "I'll be waitin' up at heaven . . ."

It didn't matter that she couldn't see him. She knew. Her words, her voice, would stay with him in the coming days, and would remain with him as he entered the afterlife and returned to Earth to guide his charges. No matter what happened, a part of her would always be with him, just as it was for her.

She sang, her heart full . . . and free.

Chapter
11

Cole paced like a caged animal in the confines of Penny Day Matthews's abandoned home. It was the night of the big wrap party for the film Paige had been making with Osiris, and if the plan they had put together with the new information Paige had secured panned out, it would be their last night in 1942.

He'd had no choice but to lay low in the days following the "negotiation" with Hawkins that had gone so terribly wrong. He was more vulnerable than he had ever been before. So he had to stay out of sight.

Or so the Charmed Ones kept telling him.

Naturally there was some risk. Ned had dropped Paige off at the inexpensive and out-of-the-way bungalow where Penny had been staying a couple of times over the last several months. He had always been a gentleman, walking her to the door, then departing without even hinting that he wanted to be let inside. Considering Hawkins's recent loss, and his grief, it didn't seem likely that he would push for a tour of the place now. And that made these narrow rooms safe.

Cole heard a sound from the living room. He looked at the clock. It was just after eight. Paige had already broken away from the party a couple of times and orbed in and out, quickly dropping off his dinner and keeping him apprised of their progress. But she wasn't due home for hours. Had something gone wrong?

Did they need him?

He rushed into the living room and was surprised to see Ned and four of his thugs waiting for him.

There were no threats. No stating of the obvious. Two more of Ned's guys shimmered in behind Cole, grabbing at him while Ned looked on with a cold, merciless gaze.

Cole knew he had only one chance to save himself. Despite Phoebe's urgings, he had left the bungalow twice and had managed to secure a certain something that just might help in a battle with the seemingly impossible-to-defeat luck demons. But if he played his hand now, he would risk denying his love and her sisters any chance of winning against Hawkins.

He stood still, letting two of the demons pin his arms to his sides while two more took turns landing punishing blows on his face, then punches and kicks to his upper body. He crumpled, and they let him fall to the floor, defenseless against their attack.

As a steel-toed shoe connected with his forehead, sending him to the depths of darkness, Cole prayed that he had played the odds in this situation just right, and that, for once, they might all get lucky going up against these guys.

Then he sank to the floor, unconscious.

Paige had been at the wrap party for hours. She laughed and mingled with dozens of people who had gathered around the partially struck sets in the center of the warehouse that was home to Osiris's latest production. Most held champagne glasses, which they had raised a short time ago, when Oscar had made a toast to the future of his company. Now the party was winding down, the time of food, drink, and dancing coming to an end, and people were approaching Oscar one at a time to tell him how much they had enjoyed working with him and how they hoped to work with him again in the near future. A few, like her, had been offered immediate work on his international presentations, and they approached Oscar differently, with far less worry. It made sense. They knew where their next meal was coming from. The others didn't. It was a strange and bittersweet time, a celebration laced with victory and sadness.

Freddy hadn't even shown up, which suited everyone just fine. He had shot his last scene the previous day, and had hobbled out without a word of thanks to anyone—typical, for him.

As she watched people approach Oscar to say their good-byes, Paige felt a little guilty. She had been offered an opportunity many would kill to have presented to them, and she was going to turn it down. She had to say no to Oscar's offer, of course, but she couldn't exactly tell him why.

And so she stood in the midst of the partyers, enjoying herself, but feeling a measure of sadness, too. Phrases like "Every ending is a new beginning" went through her mind, but words like that brought little comfort. She would genuinely miss the friends she had made at the production company.

Young Chloe came up to Paige with wide, sad, doelike eyes. Paige gave Chloe a hug, and said, "Don't worry. Everything's going to be okay."

Chloe had been selected to travel with Oscar on his overseas mission, and the Charmed Ones were confident that they would put an end to Hawkins and his plans tonight.

Yet Chloe couldn't take her eyes off Paige, who held herself with the smiling grace of someone born to be in the spotlight.

"I won't see any of you after tonight, will I?" Chloe asked.

Paige wasn't about to lie to her. "No, sweetie. I don't think so."

Paige hugged Chloe again, then watched as the girl went up to Oscar and gave him a kiss on the cheek. Chloe turned back to Paige for one final smile, then crossed the warehouse and left.

Oscar popped the cork on the last bottle of champagne as Paige approached him, forcing her to leap back, laughing as the bubbly threatened to spray all over her pretty red strapless dress.

Paige gazed into Oscar's eyes and said softly, "I'm going to miss you."

He seemed surprised. Paige hadn't said if she was going with him on his overseas venture or not, but they had been proceeding as if she were. "You're not accepting my offer?"

"I'm sorry," she said. "I've got some family business I need to take care of, stuff that can't be put off. But don't sweat it, I sent a telegram to a friend, and she'll be here to cover for me. Her name is Theda McFey. I'm hoping you've heard of her."

When Paige mentioned Theda's name, the studio owner's face lit up. "I have. I've actually approached her about parts in the past. Theda will do an excellent job, I'm sure. But I will miss you."

Paige's eyes filled with tears as she gave him a hug, and saw Ned watching her from across the room. She kissed Oscar on the cheek, then went over to Ned.

"Sorry I wasn't here sooner," he said. "I had some last-minute details to tie up."

"That's okay," she said warily, cutting a glance in Oscar's direction, then fixing her molten stare on Ned.

"I want you to know something," he said softly. "I know we had a deal. I was supposed to go easy on Oscar."

"Uh-huh."

"Well, I didn't do that."

She tensed.

"I went one better. I laid off completely and found another way to take care of the business I wanted Oscar's help on."

"Really?" Paige asked, thinking about how his words *kind* of tracked with the information she had found in his study . . . and yet was still a complete lie.

"You mean the world to me," he said, his features softening, his tone seemingly genuine. "This week I had to say good-bye to one person who was very important to me. I'd like to *not* make it two for two."

Wow, she thought. *He really means it. In his way, he really does.*

"Can I walk you out?" Ned said, offering his arm to the lady. "The night's still young. I know a bistro across town that just opened and I think you would love. Or we could go dancing. I know you love to go dancing."

She went outside, still clinging to his arm.

They walked to his shiny black Cadillac, the evening breeze clinging to them. She knew exactly how she should play this scene, but she couldn't quite resist the chance to make up a couple of new lines.

"So, you don't have anything else to do tonight?" she asked, her heart thundering. "You could really take the whole night off?"

"The whole night," he said without hesitation, staring into her eyes with something that might have been love.

It seemed that it was all up to her now. She knew full well what Ned was planning to do tonight. If he was willing to alter his plans for her, did that mean there was some chance he just might be redeemed one day?

But what about her sisters?

"I'd better take a raincheck," she said, kissing him on the cheek. "I'm sorry."

He held her close and whispered, "No, I'm sorry. They say 'luck be a lady,' right? I guess mine's just run out."

Parting from her, he smiled sadly and got inside the Cadillac.

She watched him go, then looked around and hurried to the darkened hallway of a building across the street. Piper was already there. Phoebe joined them a few minutes later.

Together they waited in darkness and in silence, as one by one, every employee of Osiris left the studio. When Paige was sure the party had ended and the place was abandoned, she took her sisters' hands and orbed them back inside.

Piper looked at her watch, a patch of moon-light coming through a high window filling its surface. "It probably won't be long now."

They took their positions and settled in.

Ten minutes later heavy doors creaked open and footsteps sounded within the studio. A small group of men entered, and some lights were turned on.

Paige recognized Ned and his men, along with the guy who was with them: Tom Phillips, the propmaster who would be traveling with Oscar for his presentations. Ned's men carried heavy crates, which they set down gently and began to open. In the meantime Tom was bring-ing a pushcart around that was loaded with boxes filled with props for the "give 'em a show" exhibitions Oscar had planned. There were swords and smaller blades for a proposed Egyptian epic, jewelry and pendants of every kind that would serve in a movie set in Britain's Buckingham Palace, and other items that would fit perfectly with the switch Ned had planned.

Sure, he had stopped going after Oscar. Why go crazy trying to convince the Big Guy to go along with things when he could achieve the same end more easily and covertly simply by getting the propmaster in his pocket?

All the Charmed Ones had to do was keep to

their hiding places and pay careful attention to exactly what props were taken and replaced by the items Ned had brought with him. Then, when everyone had gone, they could simply take the artifacts, call for a taxi (keeping in mind Cole's warning about the dire consequences of using magic in conjunction with these insanely powerful artifacts), and bring the loot to Cole, who said he knew how to siphon off enough of their power to get the time travelers all home.

Taking on Hawkins in another fight was crazy. Only Phoebe had been able to hold her own against them. The others would easily fall prey to the luck powers of their opponents.

Phoebe nudged Piper in the darkness and smiled. "You know what?" she whispered, her teeth gleaming as she smiled happily. "For the first time in I don't know *how* long, I'm actually feeling pretty lucky tonight."

"You shouldn't," a man said from just behind her. The two witches tried to bolt to their feet before Hawkins's men could grab them, but they were too slow. The demons covered Piper and Phoebe's mouths and held their arms at their sides as they hauled the witches out into the light. Paige had already been captured separately, and Cole lay at Ned Hawkins's feet, bloody and bruised, moaning and barely conscious. Tom, the propmaster, was nowhere to be seen.

It was a trap.

"So, the three of you were Cole Turner's muscle, huh?" Ned mused sadly. "The outfits were great, I gotta tell ya."

"Leave them alone," Cole managed weakly.

Ned kicked him once in the ribs, shutting him up. He turned to Paige. "If you four hadn't gone after Banzaf, I don't think I ever would have put it together. But you were the one and only person I ever mentioned his true name around, and without that, you witches could never have controlled him the way you did."

Paige tried to look away, but Ned gestured and his thug forced Paige's head in the demon's direction.

"I didn't want to believe it," Ned said mournfully. "That's why I left my study unlocked and put those papers right where I was sure you'd find them. You even left a light on to let me know you were there."

Paige and the other witches struggled as Ned drew a sharp dagger from one of the boxes he had brought. "I'm sorry about this," he said. "I really meant what I said tonight. I was hoping you'd say yes. I really was. Of course, I still would have had my guys come here and make the switch. None of us can deny our true nature. Demons are all about power and evil. So be it. 'And never suffer a witch to live.'"

Phoebe was surprised to find herself staring down at Cole, even as Hawkins was about to plunge a dagger in her half sister's heart. He was mouthing something. Finally she understood.

Jacket. Pocket.

Biting the hand of the demon who held her, Phoebe gasped for air as the smelly, meaty hand was withdrawn with a yelp of anger and surprise. She yelled, "Wait!"

Ned Hawkins glared at her. She nodded down at Cole. "Okay, we can't fight you. We know that. But that louse down there is my ex-husband. And if there's one thing I'd love to see before I die, it's his face as I finally get to kick his teeth in. Come on. What can it hurt?"

A thin, pale smile broke over the otherwise impassive mask Hawkins had adopted when he had moved to run Paige through with the blade.

"Why not?" he asked. "I only kept him alive so the three of you would see it was pointless to struggle. And so I could rip him to pieces a little at a time until I get bored with hearing him scream. Go ahead."

The thugs holding Phoebe let go of her. Shuddering, she went to Cole, who dragged himself to his knees, then stood on two wobbly legs to face her.

He smiled, blood leaking from the corner of his mouth. "Did I ever tell you how much I can't *stand* your family?"

Phoebe hauled off and delivered a stinging, crackling uppercut that snapped Cole's head back and made him sag into her arms like an empty sack. Two of Hawkins's guys rushed forward to drag him off of her just as she dug into his jacket pocket and snatched three small vials filled with crimson liquid.

Potions.

Head lolling, Cole said, "Sorry, Phoebes. I know you told me not to go out, but I just couldn't help it. Got some insurance for the three of you."

"Hold on," Hawkins said, looking at the objects in Phoebe's hand with suspicion. He aimed his blade at her and called to his men, "Don't let her throw them!"

Phoebe was about to hurl the first potion at Hawkins when she caught a small shake of the head from Cole. There were only three potions.

Three sisters.

There was no time to question. She may not have loved Cole anymore, and she may desperately have not wanted to trust him, but what choice did she have?

Phoebe threw the first vial at Paige's feet. It smashed and vapors rose up, engulfing her as Hawkins's men drew back in fear. She did the same with Piper, then herself.

The mist from the potions swept over her, and she felt it sinking into her body, her soul, changing her somehow.

"What'd you do?" Ned demanded, grabbing Cole by the lapels.

"You'll see," Cole said. He looked to Phoebe.

"Hon? Do me a favor? Hurt these guys really badly, will you?"

Phoebe felt the mist course through her, and she had a feeling that honoring Cole's request would now be possible for all three of the Charmed Ones.

Without another word, she leaped at the demons!

Chapter
12

Piper took the lead and used her powers to explode a large light positioned next to one of the demons. It rained glass and sparks onto the demon, who screamed in pain as the glass slashed his face and hands.

"Want a light?" asked Piper.

"They're only witches!" shouted Ned. He pointed at Piper. "I'll take care of this one. You boys get the other two!"

A pair of demons went after Paige. The first demon levitated a huge motion picture camera and launched it at her. The second demon positioned himself behind her to ensure that she did not get out of the way. But before Paige could orb, the camera flew around her, hit the second demon squarely in the chest, and threw him back fifty feet.

"I guess the camera just doesn't love you, huh?" quipped Paige.

Another two demons went after Phoebe. She levitated out of their reach and launched herself up to the catwalk on the second level. Another demon sent out a bolt of lightning from his fingertips to her back, but instead of hitting the Charmed One, it ricocheted off the guard railing and fried yet another demon.

The demon whose lightning bolts had gone astray shimmered out of existence, while above, Phoebe raced across the catwalk. When she was only halfway across, the demon who had targeted her rematerialized directly in front of her, blocking her way across.

"Time to get into the swing of things," said Phoebe. She turned, grabbed one of the ropes that hung from the rafters of the studio, and sailed over to the other side of the second level's landing.

Growling with frustration, the demon, intent on making up for his earlier mistake by taking the witch's lead, lunged at her but miscalculated the distance. Slamming into the warehouse wall, he fell back, leaving an impression of himself in the concrete. He plummeted to the floor and landed with a loud, angry thump.

Meanwhile Piper had her hands full. Ned had grabbed a stack of enormous film canisters and was hurtling them at the petite brunette. Fortunately she was able to explode each one before it came anywhere near her.

"Will you stop doing that!" shouted Ned, beginning to lose his patience.

"Sure, as soon as you stop throwing them at me!" shouted Piper.

Then Ned noticed that Piper was standing right in the midst of a tangle of wires. If he used his luck powers correctly, he could trip up the witch and run her through with the mystical blade he had taken from his collection of artifacts. Then his immediate problem would be solved. He willed the thick wires around Piper's feet to wrap themselves around the Charmed One, and smiled as he heard them coiling like snakes. Then he gasped as he unexpectedly found himself in the hold of wires. They had wrapped around *his* legs instead. The head demon fell face first onto the hard concrete floor of the studio.

Ned had no idea what was going on! Why wasn't their magic working properly? Once he got free of the wires, he ran over to Cole and pulled him to his feet, demanding to know what he had done.

Cole laughed in his face.

"You think I'm going to tell you? I'm having way too much fun!" said Cole.

Ned punched Cole hard in the face. Head lolling, Cole spit blood right back at the demon. Ned dropped him, wiping the blood from his eye. "That's it! I'm gonna kill you right now!"

Phoebe, still on the second level, gazed down at the events below. Why was Cole trying to provoke this demon? He could easily be killed. Phoebe levitated back down to the first level, grabbed one of the large boom microphones from the wall, and swung with all her strength at the back of Ned's head.

The force was strong enough to throw Ned forward and right into Cole's waiting fist.

"Thanks, honey!" said Cole, winking at her.

"Don't call me that!" Phoebe shouted as she went back to dealing with the other demons.

Smiling stupidly, the weakened Cole collapsed once more.

In the far corner of the studio Paige was trapped by another pair of Hawkins's demons. She almost wished they would just transform and show a more sinister face, as Cole would when he had become Belthazor. The sameness of these guys was unnerving—the gray-blue eyes, the sandy hair, the sharp, swingin' fashion sense displayed in their custom-tailored suits. It was only with great effort that she could tell any of them apart. And a part of her still didn't want to vanquish Ned, not if she could help it.

The demons released a rain spell on Paige, hoping to dampen the witch's spirits, but their magic again had the opposite effect of what they had desired. Rain shot down in a violent downpour only on the two demons, no matter where they went in the studio.

All three sisters watched and laughed as the demons tried and failed to outrun the rumbling storm clouds that followed them. The Charmed

Ones had no idea what was in those potions Cole had acquired for them, but this was starting to be fun.

Two more demons, both looking like body-builders, went for the heavy artillery and cast a tornado spell. All of the demons, Ned included, were picked up by the tornado and thrown around the studio. The tornado also swept through the wardrobe and makeup rooms on the second floor. By the time the spell had run its course, every demon, including Ned, had been covered in various forms of makeup and hair products, and finished off with some very unusual attire. The dazed Ned was tossed to the floor with a feather boa wrapped around his neck and pink fluffy slippers on his feet. Two of his men now wore dresses.

The entire studio was a disaster area. The thin walls of the sets were scattered by the tornado. But strangely enough, none of the Charmed Ones or Cole were injured in the slightest by the gale-force winds.

"When are these demons going to learn that their magic isn't working properly and just give it up," Paige said, vexed.

Suddenly Ned sprang up from a pile of harem costumes. He looked furious. His lips were moving as he said a spell to himself.

The Charmed Ones could feel the power coalescing inside the studio in answer to Ned's spell.

"Ned, don't do this!" Paige called. "Just walk away. Please!"

He tossed the knife at her, and it might have sunk right into her heart if yet another light from the rigging above hadn't fallen and deflected it at exactly the right instant.

"All right," she said. "That's how it is."

"I think it's time to take cover," said Piper.

"I agree," said Phoebe, nodding. She grabbed Cole and they all ran for the huge doors of the studio to get outside and away from Ned and whatever spell he was casting.

The walls of the studio shook and seemed to bend inward as if they were being pulled toward Ned by some unstoppable force.

The four figures ran into the studio office in the building next door and held their breath. The three sisters held on to one another, with Cole in the middle to protect him from whatever was happening. There was a huge *whoosh* and then everything was silent. The Charmed Ones waited to make sure it was over, then carefully went outside with Cole following.

The entire building that had housed the soundstage of Osiris Studios had been leveled. It was like the structure had just collapsed in on itself. Somewhere underneath all that rubble was Ned Hawkins and his gang . . . and the artifacts.

"Ned must have destroyed the entire building trying to get to us," said Paige.

"Luckily he wasn't able to create a binding spell to keep us inside the building along with him," said Phoebe.

"Yeah, that *is* lucky," said Cole with a mischievous look on his face.

"What exactly were those potions that you had us use on ourselves?" Phoebe asked Cole.

Cole laughed. "I got to thinking. You know that old saying, 'If it weren't for bad luck, I wouldn't have any luck at all'?"

"It was bad luck," Phoebe said. "We already had been dosed with bad luck, so when Hawkins tried to use his magic to make our luck turn rotten, the two just canceled each other out."

"Pretty smart, huh?" Cole asked. "You were the one who gave me the idea. Back in that alley, you were the only one who wasn't affected by Hawkins and his bad luck mojo. I kept thinking about why that would have been. Then it came to me: You were already having a string of bad luck, as far as you were concerned. You'd fallen for the bait the luck demons had set out in our time. You've been stuck with me when you would have rather I'd stayed in some hell dimension the rest of eternity. It just all made sense."

They went back, climbing into the rubble, and started digging for the artifacts. Fortunately the crates were all in a single cluster, and they uncovered them easily. It wouldn't be long before someone happened by who would call for the police and rescue units.

"Phoebe, can I have a moment?" Cole asked, still wincing with pain as he made the slightest movement. She followed him to a spot a few yards from the rubble.

"Phoebe, I want you to listen to me, please. We've got a chance here."

"What are you *raving* about?"

He gestured at the expanse of mystical loot. "These guys are idiots. They don't know what they've got here, they don't have the first clue about real power. But I do. Imagine the good the two of us could do if we took these things for ourselves. We could be together. We could make the world better!"

"That's not what they're meant to do. They're not meant for manipulation of good or evil."

"Just, please, consider it."

"Can these things get us back to our time or not?"

He nodded sharply. "Not."

Phoebe's face fell. "Excuse me? But you said—"

"All right, technically, yes, they can. They've got the power. But power isn't everything, and we're talking about the flow of history. Every one of these items is earmarked for a specific destiny. Time is pretty resilient, it really is." He shuddered. "What I'm trying to say is, for the most part, our timeline can handle a few minor changes here and there. Going back and taking out Hitler before he came to power, no, that would pretty much create a whole new world, change the timeline completely. And it usually takes something of that magnitude to create ripples with that kind of impact."

"And using these to send us back would qualify."

"Yes. You three could go back, but it wouldn't be the world you knew. You'd be outside of any changes that happened, you'd be the same, even though, technically, you might not even be born in the new timeline, or there might be another you, it's hard to say. But the changes would be big. These things are all meant to do good in the world. And I know all the details. Places, times, all of it. I also know all the close calls, all the missed opportunities, all the evil that happens because these things weren't used when they might have been, or as well as they could have been. Look at this."

He held up a pin no bigger than a tie clasp that he had taken from one of the crates. Hooking it onto his lapel, he threw open his hands. "There we go. Complete sixth sense where danger's involved. Just like Spider-Man. Tack this thing onto JFK's jacket, or Martin Luther King's necktie, and it all comes out differently. Or we could make it so much better even before then. We could end this war tomorrow."

The other two witches had gravitated over and heard a good chunk of Cole's pitch. He looked to Piper for support. "Leo wouldn't have to die."

Piper hugged herself. "If he never died, he never would have come to me. Some things, even bad things, are meant to be, Cole. We have no right changing them."

"But people wouldn't have to go hungry or be oppressed. I'm talking absolute power here."

Phoebe's gaze narrowed. "Good. A former demon wanting to play God? Good or evil, Cole, none of us has the right to control anything absolutely and totally."

"Phoebe, please," Cole said, grabbing her arms. "We're stuck here anyway. Why don't we—"

He broke off suddenly, a strange look coming over him. "Danger," he said hoarsely, the pin on his suit casting a dull crimson glow. "Get down!"

A figure exploded out of the rubble, leaping high into the air, and landing with a nasty hiss. Cole, who stood closest, was tossed from his feet, and when he landed, the small pin that had alerted him to danger slipped from his lapel and sank into the rubble.

The figure that had appeared was Ned Hawkins. Only he was different now. His face was black and charred, his gray-blue eyes incandescent in the moonlight, his teeth needle sharp. His jacket had been torn from him, and he stood in his suit pants and a shredded white shirt stained with his own blood. His bare feet showed curling talons instead of toes.

He pointed at Paige. "You did this to me! You made me show my true face!"

"Uh-huh," Paige said wearily, crossing the wreckage and yanking a sword from the boxes of powerful artifacts.

"What are you gonna do with that?" Ned asked. "Try to use your magic with it and you'll create a backlash that'll rip this continent in half!"

"He's right," Cole warned. "And it won't work for you otherwise. There are all kinds of rituals and wards you have to enact first and—"

"Yeah, yeah," Paige said. "I'm sure."

And she was. She could feel the sword's power. It thirsted for blood, it wanted her to call upon its magic.

It didn't care about the consequences.

"That . . . won't . . . work!" Ned hissed, shaking his head as if he were speaking to a foolish child.

With a grunt of effort, she spun and rammed it through Ned's chest, impaling the gasping, startled demon. Trembling, he grasped at the metal jutting from his chest, then dropped to the debris-strewn lot, still staring at the weapon in open disbelief.

"Swords *always* work, pal," Paige said.

Phoebe and Piper stared at her, open-mouthed. Cole snickered and said, "Remind me not to get you that mad at me."

"I think I just did," Paige said. She looked

around, then gestured at the crates with the artifacts. "We've got to get these things out of here
before anyone shows up."

"Wait, there's that spell of Theda's," Phoebe
said. "It puts things back the way they were."

"Only inanimate objects," Piper said.

Paige looked around. "Sounds good to me.
I'm not sure if poor Oscar has insurance for this
kind of thing or not!"

The witches joined hands, making it a Power
of Three spell. They chanted:

> *Return, return, the form that was,*
> *reshape, retake, we ask because,*
> *much good will come, much evil flee,*
> *return, return, 'twas meant to be . . .*

In seconds the whirling winds that had caused
so much damage were alive again, lifting huge
chunks of battered wood, metal, brick, and more
into the air. Girders moaned and lifted themselves from the destruction, and quickly, piece by
piece, the building restored itself, the walls jam-
ming into place, the ceiling covering them, the
lights, the sets, and every little bit of ruptured
material fusing together magically.

In moments Osiris was reborn.

"Interesting . . . trick . . . ," a hoarse voice
called.

The Charmed Ones and Cole turned to see
Ned Hawkins back on his feet, still desperately

clutching the magical sword that was trying to yank itself out of his chest and return to the crate from which Paige had pulled it.

"Oh," Paige whispered. "The sword. We used magic on the sword."

"Doesn't that mean cataclysmic disaster now?" Phoebe said hoarsely.

Cole nodded. "Pretty much."

"Just checking."

Violet energies with swirling white lines of luminescence leaped from the sword and shot upward, threatening to tear the roof of the newly restored studio.

Suddenly a booming voice said, *"No."*

The walls literally shook with the power of that voice, and the funnel of dark energies surging from the sword stayed where they were, inches away from the ceiling. Yet they weren't frozen, the spiraling light could still be seen in the dark mass.

A figure fully two stories high was partially revealed behind the sword's great energies. Paige could see a great arm reaching out, a hand covering the funnel from the sword, a face that seemed ancient and wise, and a chest that would have made Adonis sick with envy.

"Woo!" she called. "What's this now?"

"By the gods," Piper whispered.

"Yeah, I'd say he's one of them," Cole said. "A god of luck would be my guess."

Hawkins looked back, trembling in terror.

"No. We broke away. We worship you no more. This is our time, our chance to be free!"

"It's a lack of vision that keeps you and all of your kind from becoming anything more," the giant said. A dozen cloaked demons appeared, surrounding him. They looked just like the uglies the luck demons in the present had tricked the Charmed Ones into fighting. *"My emissaries, those who watch, have now seen all they must. They will benefit from your errors, and gain the widom and power that might have come to you and all of your line.*

"My emissaries, those you see here, will now be the Lords of the Outer Dark, and you, Ned Hawkins, as true name will forever be denied your kind, will be remembered as the one who brought misfortune and ruin upon your people. That is your legacy."

Piper set her hands on her hips. "Hey, Mr. God Person or whatever you are!"

"I have had many names in this and many other worlds. Luck is my dominion."

"Great. Lucky, thanks, nice to meet ya." She pointed at the funnel of dark energies that the giant was holding down. "Listen, we messed up, we know, and you're here 'cause old Ned and the rest like him deserve a good slapping. Fine. But since you never would have found him unless we'd let loose all this power around him, do you think, since you're here anyway, you could do something with that black funnely thing so it doesn't rip apart half the world or whatever? We'd really appreciate it."

"*Your point is sound. You've done me a service and I owe you a boon. Saving the lives of all around you is something that is within you—it is simply who you are, what you do. I can sense that. But what is it you want, for yourselves?*"

"Just to go home," Paige said. "Back to our own time."

The giant nodded, and the funnel of energy was ripped from Ned and the sword. It sped across the studio, changing shape, turning into a spiraling vortex similar to the one that had brought them here.

"See?" Piper said, tossing up one hand. "Who says it doesn't pay just to ask for what you want?"

"*Farewell,*" the giant roared, grasping Hawkins's screaming, flailing form, and hauling him away as he disappeared with the cloaked demons.

The sword that had been driven into Hawkins's chest clanked noisily to the floor.

"That's it," Cole said. "There's the way home. See? I knew we'd find it."

Phoebe glared at him.

"Just one thing." Cole crossed the studio and stood beside the great objects of power. "We can't just leave these things lying around. Someone's got to make sure they don't fall into the wrong hands, and we sure can't use magic on them— you saw what almost happened a second ago."

The witches eyed the vortex. There was no telling how long it would remain open.

Phoebe spoke first. "It's your choice, Cole. If

those things are what's important to you, if it's power that you're looking for—"

"Cut it out, Phoebe," Cole said. "If I want power, all I have to do is get inside that vortex with you. Back home, I've got more than I know what to do with. I'm saying I'll stay here. And I'll make sure that what destiny had in mind for these things is what happens to them. If you go back and I start changing things here, you might never be born. I couldn't live with that. I love you, Phoebe. If I do this, I'd be doing it for you. What do you say?"

Piper crossed her arms over her chest. "I don't believe I'm saying this, but I think he actually means it."

Across from them, the vortex shuddered, growing wider, then more narrow, and finally blinking in and out of view several times as it started to become unstable.

"You don't have much time. Go!" Cole hollered.

The soft tap of rapidly approaching footfalls made them all turn. It was Tom, the propmaster.

"Go ahead," he said. "Go back to your own time. I'll take care of things here."

Phoebe's brow furrowed in surprise. "But I thought you were in it with Hawkins!"

Spreading his hands, Tom was encased by streaks of white light, and chimes sounded as he orbed from his end of the studio to right next to the Charmed Ones.

"You're a Whitelighter!" Paige said.

Tom nodded. "The Elders sent me to watch over Chloe. I ended up realizing the best way to keep her safe was trying to put a stop to this business with Hawkins and his crew. I didn't know you four were going to show up. Truth is, without what you did, I don't think I would have had much of a chance of stopping those guys. I didn't realize how powerful they really were. But I can certainly take it from here."

The vortex winked in and out of existence again. Cole joined the Charmed Ones, and together they walked into the opening between moments of time and space, the power of the vortex swallowing them whole.

Leo paced near the spot where his wife, her sisters, and that creep Cole had been yanked away. He had wanted to go consult the Elders. But Piper might find a way to get a message to him, and if he strayed too far, and missed it. . . . He couldn't go, he just couldn't!

A sudden heat rose up at his back. He spun and found himself face to face with the luck demons who had been behind this all along.

"A Whitelighter. Isn't that interesting, Mr. Sigh?" one said.

"Indeed, Mr. Tremble. He seems troubled. I think we should put him out of his misery."

"A fine idea, Mr. Sigh. A fine idea."

Leo's gaze narrowed. "You want to fight? Fine. Then maybe, after I'm done hitting both of you so hard your mothers can feel it, you'll tell me how I can get Piper back!"

The faces of the luck demon's paled, and a strange violet light washed over them as their shadows raced back across the banks of San Francisco Bay. Leo sensed something behind him.

"Leo, move, now!" Piper commanded.

Grinning ear to ear, Leo backed off, looking to one side to see a new vortex disappearing on the platform, the Charmed Ones and Cole standing before it.

Mr. Sigh trembled. "Wait a second . . . they're back!"

"That can't be." Mr. Tremble sighed.

Cole smiled. "Yeah, tough break, fellas. It looks like your luck just ran out."

Standing back, Cole took great delight in watching the Charmed Ones clasp hands and chant a spell Theda had given to them:

> *In darkness and in light*
> *Your evil we will fight*
> *As you have doomed so many souls*
> *This spell will blow you full of holes!*

The demons who had very nearly destroyed them all screamed and exploded as a hailstorm of fiery energies cut through them!

They had been vanquished.

"Still had enough of that potion on us to take down their sorry butts, I guess," Phoebe said.

Cole turned to Phoebe. He had allowed himself the slightest hope that all he had done would mean something to her, that there might still be some chance to make her believe he had changed. "The other night you said I might get a little gratitude from you when I've earned it."

She looked away. "Yep. That's what I said."

"So, Phoebes . . . have I earned it?"

She stared at him for a very long time. Then, sighing wearily, she turned from him and said sadly, "Ask me again in another sixty years."

Ahead, Piper ran to her beloved, who caught her up and swung her around, his relief the most powerful force she had encountered yet—other than her own, of course.

"Piper, sweetheart," Leo whispered, holding her tight.

All she could do was bury her face in his shoulder and appreciate this moment in time, and every moment she got to spend with him, as the miracle it was.

Cole watched them, then turned from Phoebe. Who knew what the future held for them?

He shimmered away.

Moments later Phoebe and Paige were walking down the beach, enjoying the lights of their own time, which sparkled along the waterfront.

"So, what are you going to do?" Phoebe asked.

"Besides orbing us home and changing out of these clothes?" Paige remembered giving her number to that cute guy at the library. "Who knows? A girl just might get lucky!"

"Why don't you go on ahead," Phoebe suggested warmly. "I feel like a walk on the beach is just what I need right now. I'll either call for Leo, or get a cab, when I'm ready."

"Okay!" Paige said brightly. She winked, gave her sister a quick kiss, and orbed into the night.

Phoebe looked up at the stars. She was back in her own time and her family was safe. What more could she really want?

Smiling, she thought, *Maybe it's a lucky night for all of us.*

She walked down the shore, feeling happy and free for the first time in ages.

BASED ON THE HIT TV SERIES

A magical incantation invokes in the three Halliwell sisters powers they've never dreamed of. As the Charmed Ones, they are witches charged with protecting innocents.

But when Prue is killed at the hands of the Source, Piper and Phoebe believe the Power of Three to be broken.

That is, until their half-sister, Paige Matthews, arrives at the Manor, with a few tricks—and a few questions—of her own....

Look for a new title every other month! Original novels based on the hit television series created by Constance M. Burge.

Available from Simon & Schuster

2387

. . . A GIRL BOR[N]

WITHOUT THE FEAR [OF]

FEARLESS™

A SERIES BY
FRANCINE PASCAL

PUBLISHED BY SIMON & SCHUSTER

When I was six months old, I dropped from the sky—
lone survivor of a deadly Japanese plane crash.
newspapers named me Heaven. I was adopted by
wealthy family in Tokyo, pampered, and protected.
nineteen years, I thought I was lucky.
I'm learning how wrong I was.

I've lost the person I love most.
I've begun to uncover the truth about my family.
Now I'm being hunted. I must fight back, or die.
The old Heaven is gone.

I AM SAMURAI GIRL.

A new series from Simon Pulse

The Book of the Sword
The Book of the Shadow

BY CARRIE ASAI

Available in bookstores now

侍